BLIGHTED INHERITANCE

Following her father's murder, Leonora Mayfield disguises herself as a maid-servant in order to seek proof of a large amount of money owed by her father's employer, Sir Francis Carrock. She is determined to dislike and distrust her father's successor, Adam Rigton, but her search proves more difficult than expected and she is reluctantly becoming attracted to Adam. Is there more than a debt at stake and has she unknowingly placed herself and younger brother, Robert, in grave danger?

Books by Anne Hewland
in the Linford Romance Library:

STOLEN SECRET
TO TRUST A STRANGER
A SUBTLE DECEIT

ANNE HEWLAND

BLIGHTED INHERITANCE

Complete and Unabridged

LINFORD
Leicester

First published in Great Britain in 2009

First Linford Edition
published 2010

British Library CIP Data

Hewland, Anne.
  Blighted inheritance. - -
  (Linford romance library)
  1. Love stories.
  2. Large type books.
  I. Title II. Series
  823.9'2–dc22

  ISBN 978–1–44480–182–8

Published by
F. A. Thorpe (Publishing)
Anstey, Leicestershire

Set by Words & Graphics Ltd.
Anstey, Leicestershire
Printed and bound in Great Britain by
T. J. International Ltd., Padstow, Cornwall

This book is printed on acid-free paper

1

She stared into the cold eyes of the elderly man sitting in front of her. Desperation had driven Leonora Mayfield to the grey stone splendour of Carrock Hall; she had hardly thought she would be granted a direct interview with Sir Francis Carrock, the most powerful man in the county of Cumbria for as long as Leonora could remember.

The wine-red brocade of his coat emphasised the pallor of his cruel face. She wondered now whether she had been foolish to come. She resisted the temptation to twist her fingers in the dark curls that fell to her shoulders, escaping her cap. A bad habit her father had always said. If she even blinked, she knew she would weep. And she must not. She must stay strong for the sake of Robert and little Sophy.

She prayed that her voice would not

betray her. 'It is bad enough that our father lies dead — murdered. But now you wish to compound our misery by refusing to pay the money you owe him?' She swallowed hard. 'The expenses incurred by my father during the election — on your behalf.'

Sir Francis made a play of examining a fine silver snuff box, holding it up to the light. 'Miss Mayfield, think yourself fortunate that I have not demanded the money that was allegedly stolen from my agent — your father — during the attack. As you know, this was the rents that he had collected for a number of my properties. I would be within my rights to demand that you make good my loss.'

Leonora stared at him in horror. 'How can we?'

'Of course. You cannot. So I am willing to overlook that. As to money owed — I have no recollection of any such. An amount was certainly repaid to your father within months of the election.'

She should have known how it would be. But she had had to try. The sum owing would make all the difference to them now they were alone. 'Some was repaid, yes. But by no means all. My father had the tallies in question and was about to present them to you.' She shivered as she saw that Sir Francis was no longer smiling.

'I have been over-generous in allowing you to speak to me in person. And even before your father's funeral has taken place which is hardly fitting. I suggest that you relay your misplaced concerns to a suitable male relative who may discuss this on your behalf. If he so wishes.'

'There is no one living here. We have only my father's cousin who lives in Yorkshire.' As Sir Francis well knew; she was certain of that. Besides, she had little hope of Uncle Merridew achieving anything for them. She had met him only a few times and he had always seemed a man who would choose the easier route in life.

Sir Francis raised elegant brows. 'Your father's family is of little interest to me. There is no proof of this claim and although your circumstances are regrettable, they are no concern of mine.' He was studying her face intently.

'There is proof,' Leonora cried, forgetting all caution. 'I know it. And when I have made a full and complete search of my father's papers, I shall find it and bring it to you.'

Sir Francis leaned back in his chair as if satisfied. 'I am afraid you will not have that opportunity. There is no time. You see, I have my own reason for granting you this meeting. In recognition of your father's long and loyal service to me, I decided to tell you myself.' He paused, waiting for his words to have their full effect.

Leonora's hand shifted to her throat. 'Tell me what?'

'Why, that your father's successor is already appointed. My affairs cannot be kept marking time. And Carr House

— as you must know — goes with the position. You will have to vacate it as soon as possible. Following the funeral of course — I will be generous in that respect.'

In the grief and turmoil of the last few days, Leonora had never thought of this. She saw at once what a grave mistake she had made. She pictured the warm sunglow walls, the neat rows of windows on either side of the front door and felt a heartbreaking sense of loss. 'But it is our family home. We were all born here.'

'Your home no longer, I fear, for it is my house and is needed.' Sir Francis rose as he reached for the bell. 'Goodbye Miss Mayfield. My best wishes to you.' He bowed, 'And for your family's future.'

2

Aunt Merridew's tone was disdainful. 'I thought there were more. Fortunate, as it happens, that there are not.' Their father's cousin and his wife had arrived for the funeral and at Aunt Merridew's request, Leonora had brought the children to the drawing room. Uncle William Merridew cast a glance at Leonora as if pleading with her not to take offense. 'I believe several died in infancy.'

Leonora clenched her fingers behind her back but managed to say nothing. There had been no need to instruct the children to be on their best behaviour. They were shocked and subdued by all that had happened. Little Sophy had a thumb in her mouth, a habit given up in babyhood. Robert, though pale, stood staunchly, feet a little apart as befitted the new man of the house

— although but ten years old.

'This is a regrettable situation,' Aunt Merridew said, 'but I suppose it cannot be helped. William?'

'Ah, yes. We have discussed it at length. And my wife, with great generosity, has agreed to take the little girl.'

Aunt Merridew nodded graciously. 'She should fit into our nursery without too much trouble. And the boy — Robert? — he may go to live with Cousin Talbot.'

Leonora stared at her, hardly able to believe what she had just heard. Robert said, 'I won't mind it if Cousin Talbot will arrange for me to go to sea. I am to begin as a midshipman and eventually rise to Captain.'

Uncle William leaned forward. 'What is this? Is this paid for? This could solve everything.'

'My father promised,' Robert said. 'See — he carved this little ship for me, out of a bone. It is something sailors do. He said it would be a lucky charm for

7

me and when I go to sea I shall always carry it and — .'

'Hush, Robert,' Leonora said gently. She turned to face her uncle. 'No, I am afraid not, but it has long been Robert's dearest wish. My father intended to organise this for him but had not done so as yet.'

'It is all of a piece,' Aunt Merridew said crossly. 'Fortunate in that case that we made our own arrangements for you and that Cousin Talbot is already agreeable.'

'But aunt — ,' Leonora gathered her wits. 'We cannot be split up. We must stay together.'

'There is no 'must' about it. If your father had been more efficient with his affairs — but there it is.'

'It was not his fault. He never recovered from my mother's sudden death. And he had made a beginning for us in trying to regain the money owed to him by Sir Francis. And I am determined to continue. There will then be no need for the three of us to be

8

dependent on anyone else.'

'Out of the question I'm afraid,' Uncle William said, his voice gruff but not unkind. 'There is no proof of this claim. Involving lawyers would be throwing good money after bad.'

'There is proof. I am sure of it. My father as good as told me so. And given time, I can find it, I am sure.' Leonora bit back her anger. She must not antagonise them when they could be her allies in this fight.

'But Sir Francis has explained to you that you are to vacate this house.' Aunt Merridew raised her voice as if addressing an idiot. 'A pity your father had not thought to secure you a husband. That would have saved us all a great deal of trouble. Out of the question now of course. However, William has also found a place for you. Not easy for an impoverished young woman of eighteen years, I may add.'

Uncle William said quickly, 'My wife's great aunt is in need of a companion. She is almost bedridden and living alone. I know she will appreciate having a young and energetic girl to assist her.'

'A companion?' Leonora's thoughts were whirling. 'Would I be near Robert and Sophy? Could I see them frequently?'

'See them?' Aunt Merridew laughed. 'Merciful heavens — there will not be the time to spare from your duties for gadding about. Even if the distance made it possible. You will be in Shropshire and Robert in Penrith. And Sophy in Bradford with us.' She leaned forward. 'And you are not to think that you will have any expectations; my great aunt's will has been clearly made these ten years. Her fortune is left solidly to her own blood relatives. But on that understanding I believe you may do very well together. You will be fed, clothed and provided for, at least for the present. No small thing in your unfortunate circumstances.'

Sophy began to cry, 'Are you going away too, Leo? Please do not.'

Even without feeling the children's grief and horror, Leonora could not have kept silent. She ached to tell them that it was not true; that Aunt Merridew was wickedly mistaken, that the family would stay together. But already, ever since her interview with Sir Francis she had endured sleepless nights wondering how this could be possible. Much as it irked her, without the help of these relatives she could not see how the safety and well being of the younger children could be managed. She could not see them starving or homeless and on their behalf at least, the offer must be accepted. For the time being at any rate.

She knelt down, her face on a level with Sophy's. 'Aunt Merridew and Uncle William have asked you to stay for a while. It is kind of them and will be for the best. You'll see.'

'But I want to stay here. With you and Robert and Samuel and Jenny and Lucy,' Sophy said sadly.

'I am afraid we cannot. There is a

new gentleman coming here to work for Sir Francis, as our father did. This house will be his.'

'Well, I wish he would not come. I hate him!'

'Such sentiments are not fitting in one so young,' Aunt Merridew said briskly. 'Now, if all is settled, we wish to be on our way early tomorrow. I trust the child can be ready by then? And your servant is to escort the boy to Penrith.'

Dazed, Leonora went to the door and called for Lucy, the maidservant. With a few words of explanation, she gave the children into her care. 'And what are the arrangements for myself?' She felt as if she were being regarded with no more sense or feeling than a parcel.

'It is all arranged. We will transport you with us for the first thirty miles or so,' Uncle William said.

'And then you are to take the Stage, followed by the Carrier's cart from Macclesfield. Your uncle has very kindly made all the arrangements for you,' their aunt added.

Leonora stared at the self satisfied faces. Their uncle a little apologetic perhaps, but her aunt clearly pleased that an inconvenient problem had been dealt with. Well, she would not be part of their problem. She would show them that she could manage for herself.

'No.' Leonora said. 'Thank you, but I shall not be accepting your relative's offer.' She wanted to smile at the disbelief on their faces. But if she must be a companion, or a governess, she would rather have a position of her own choosing. Finding a place could not be so very difficult, surely?

Aunt Merridew's face was growing red. 'And what do you intend, pray?'

'Suffice it to say that my future will not be your responsibility. But that I shall be well provided for.' She held her head high, hoping to convince them. She had not the slightest idea what she would do but they must not suspect this. However, as she had guessed, they were only too glad to be rid of her. She said sweetly, 'This will be a relief to you surely, ma'am? And be assured, this way your 'expectations' are perfectly safe.'

★ ★ ★

The next morning came all too quickly. Leonora knew she must maintain a smiling face for the children's sake but it was all but beyond her. She was almost too tired to stand, having spent hours searching fruitlessly through her father's ledgers, with his last words ringing in her head. When he had been carried back by the farm labourers who had found him on the track way, he had been delirious with pain.

'Leonora — there are papers. I hid them. But then — too dangerous — maybe best forgotten.'

'Where?' she had whispered urgently. 'Where did you hide them?'

He shook his head, unable to say more. But she knew that they existed and would be somewhere in the house. She must find them. Who knew when she would have the chance again, if ever? Once she left Carr House, she would never have the opportunity to return. Doubtless, this was exactly what Sir Francis was hoping.

The unwelcome relatives were gone and the front door closed behind them — but her farewells to the children had been heartbreaking. Leonora had tried to conceal this new grief and remain calm and cheerful, for their sakes. At the last moment, Uncle William had decided that appearances would be better served and their duties seen to be done if their own servant was to escort Robert. Leonora suspected that the pair were considering Cousin Talbot's reaction rather than anything else. But she was glad that Samuel, the Mayfield's manservant for many years, did not have to leave for a long journey at this difficult time. Now, with the house unnaturally silent and empty, Leonora wanted only to weep herself into sleeping oblivion. But there was no time for that.

She went into the kitchen, where the three loyal servants were waiting quietly. 'I need to speak to you all.'

'As expected, Miss Leonora.' Samuel was dignified.

Lucy was more forthright. 'And we all thought you would be finding a home with your family — even though we've seen little enough of them in the past. But why have they left without you? Are you to follow on?'

'No.' Leonora must say something. 'I am to make my own way in the world. By my own choice. But first I need to talk about all of you. I cannot answer with certainty but if you stay here there is always the possibility that the new agent will retain you. I shall of course furnish you with the best references possible. You have all been so good, so loyal . . . '

'Well, I think it's shameful,' Lucy said. 'And I'm sure I don't wish to stay on for the new person. As you know, I have been training Jenny up to replace me when I leave to marry John Hesket.

She is quick and apt and can manage well enough for this new man, I'm sure. I wish to bring the wedding forward; I spoke to John a night or two back and he is agreeable.'

'Oh, Lucy.' Leonora could hardly imagine the house without her. She had been a tower of strength during the past terrible week.

'The truth is,' Lucy said, 'I don't feel I could work here for anyone else, good or bad. I shall miss you and the children so much . . . ' Her voice faltered. 'And your poor father.'

Leonora swallowed. 'And what about you, Jenny? Can you cope with this? It is only a month or so sooner than we planned.'

'Of course I can,' Jenny said. 'You and Lucy have been such good teachers. I don't mind.'

Samuel said quietly, 'And I will stay on, of course. This house has been my life for so long. Whether the new man may consider me too old — but we shall see. And you, Miss, what are you going to do? Where will you go?'

'Yes, indeed,' Lucy said quickly. 'I shan't go until I know that you are settled somewhere, Miss Leonora.'

Leonora raised her chin. Perhaps she should have been giving thought to that instead of staying awake seeking the missing papers. She only knew that she could not leave this house when the evidence she needed was somewhere within it. Surely she would find the papers before too long? There was no real need for her to leave until the new man actually arrived. Who was to know? But even so, Sir Francis had told her he would be arriving almost immediately. And he would be his employer's man, through and through, with no sympathy for her search.

Idle and foolish ideas flickered through her mind. Her father had employed a clerk at times. If only she were a man, she could have applied for such a position. As it was, there were few things she was qualified to do.

The three faces were regarding her solemnly.

She said, 'My aunt intended a position for me as nothing more than an unpaid servant. It seems to me,' she swallowed hard, 'service is a respectable and honourable occupation and I would rather be paid honestly for my labours.'

'You're never going to be a servant!' Lucy exclaimed indignantly. 'That doesn't seem right. Though I know you would be good at the work, because you're accustomed to working with us. But where would you find work? The next hiring fair is some time off.'

The idea came to Leonora like a flash of bright light. She smiled. 'There is a place here — at least for the moment. I shall take your place, Lucy! In fact, I have an idea, if you will allow it — I shall actually become you!'

It all seemed so simple. The three servants were shocked at first but were quick to rally and pledge their support. Particularly when Leonora confided in them of her quest, which would give her the independent means to reunite the little family.

'If I were to stay here in Eskthwaite, it might be difficult,' Lucy said, 'but since I am to live all but ten miles away with the hills between us, there's unlikely to be any talk.'

'All the same, I can do the greater share of the work,' Jenny said. 'It wouldn't seem right else. And it will give you time to get on with your searching. If we are seen together, you can make out to be instructing me, as Lucy would be doing.'

Samuel said, 'I doubt he'll notice the difference. A man alone, with no family — for that's the talk, miss, in the village. He'll be running his own household and won't care how things are managed as long as all runs smoothly. And we shall make sure that it does.'

'Yes,' Leonora said, 'we will handle any problems ourselves, bringing nothing to his attention.'

Lucy laughed. 'It seems strange — but it could work. And if it brings justice so you can have the children back together, it will be worth it.'

'It will be easy,' Samuel said. 'We shall all stand by you.'

Leonora could have wept again, touched by their loyalty. 'I must prepare myself. First I shall move my belongings up to the top floor with the rest of you and clear my room.'

'What are you to wear?' Jenny asked. 'Your workaday muslin would do at a pinch but still doesn't look like our clothes. The material is too fine.'

'I'll let you have something of mine,' Lucy said at once.

'Indeed not — you have very little yourself.' Leonora was suddenly inspired. 'I know — I have little enough to give you for a wedding gift now — but we could look amongst my mother's clothes in the attics and see if there is anything that would suit to fashion your wedding dress.' She brushed Lucy's protests aside. No time for weeping.

Now that she had a plan before her, Leonora felt there was a glimmer of hope to lighten her grief. This would be her aim — to gather the children together in one household so that at least they might be united in their new life. While she could keep hold of that aim, there was no time for useless tears.

The next departure was Lucy's, the following day. The maidservant left early, taking the route through the back garden and along the river bank to avoid remark, although following the search in the attics, her single customary bundle had become two. John Hesket, the young farmer she was to marry, would meet her a mile or so out of the town.

'Right,' Jenny said, briskly smoothing her apron. 'If you don't mind, Miss, I think I should clean each room as far as I may, in order to give a good impression. The grates were all cleaned first thing as usual but maybe I should lay the fires ready — there will be a chill in the air soon.'

'Of course, I only wish I had time to help. But please call me Lucy from now on,' Leonora reminded her. She felt brisk and workmanlike in the sensible grey print dress and apron Lucy had given her. 'And if the new master should think to examine the household account books where everyone employed here is listed, I shall explain that I am to leave shortly. That I am presently acting as under housemaid, in preparation for leaving you in sole charge. But as Samuel said, he is hardly likely to notice, or be interested. He will have enough to do in coming to an understanding of his duties for Sir Francis.'

Jenny sniffed. 'And I don't envy him in that.'

Perhaps they would have a day or two to get used to their new roles, Leonora thought, depending on how far the new master must travel. Leonora had turned the attentions of her search to the little used office at the rear of the house where her father's clerk had worked. But good clerks had proved hard to find; those John Mayfield had employed were often more trouble than they were worth and, since his wife's death, Mr Mayfield had managed without. Leonora had taken a broom and duster with her and these proved necessary for nothing on the shelves seemed to have been touched for months if not years, although Lucy and Jenny had dusted the plain elm wood desk and stool often enough. She dusted and swept as she replaced various items and the task proved almost soothing. A day or two like this and surely her quest would be over.

It was almost a shock when mid afternoon one set of hooves in the street outside stopped purposefully at the gate. Somehow, her senses alert, she heard the sound beyond the usual passing clatter of horses and cartwheels.

This was it. Leonora breathed deeply, trying to calm herself and got a nose full of dust for her pains. She was still trying to stifle a sneeze as Samuel went to the front door and she and Jenny went to wait in the kitchen. They had decided that unless the new master asked to meet the servants, they would not put themselves forward. Why run the risk unless he enquired about her?

Jenny smiled and patted her hand. Leonora was wishing now that they had gathered in the hall to meet him, getting the introductions over all at once. Samuel would have run through their names and the man would hardly have noticed who they were, or even cared. Too late now. So much depended on the kind of person he was.

It was no good. She had to have a look, now, while he was occupied in Samuel's welcome — and seemed to be discussing the arrangements for his horse. Samuel was saying, 'We have a small stable building at the back that will take a horse and Mr Mayfield used that on occasion but latterly he found it more convenient to keep a mount at the Town End Farm, next door. He had made a special arrangement with them there,' Samuel added.

She tiptoed to the door. 'No, miss,' Jenny hissed. 'Lucy wouldn't have allowed that.'

Too late. Leonora stared at him, mesmerised. Tall, chestnut brown hair, simply worn, firm if unsmiling features. He was glancing upwards as if taking in the proportions of the house — the hallway, the stairs, the doors leading into the front office and the dining room. Abruptly he moved his head and she found herself staring directly into his dark eyes.

She jerked back into the kitchen, seized a bowl and began stirring flour without thinking what she was doing. Samuel appeared in the doorway, sympathetic reproof in his tone. 'The new master would like to see you both now.' Leonora started and flour scattered across the kitchen table. So much for not bringing herself to his attention.

'Just say yes or no and keep your head down,' Jenny murmured. 'It will be all right.'

Leonora's thoughts were whirling.

She could hardly believe her own foolishness. Had she given herself away before she had even begun? No, keep calm — any curious maidservant might have done the same, unable to resist a first glimpse. But there must be no more such lapses.

She followed Jenny out into the hall and bobbed meekly. Not daring to look up as Samuel announced Mr Adam Rigton and told him their names. She was aware only of an imposing and shadowy figure. She must remember to answer to Lucy.

'So we have two maid servants as well as a man servant? In a house of this small size?' he asked.

'Lucy will soon be leaving us, sir, in a matter of weeks. As soon as Jenny is trained to our satisfaction.'

Would he consider Lucy a fit person to be training anyone after her regrettable mistake? She must be so careful. Already he had shown himself more knowledgeable of domestic matters than they had expected. He could dismiss her if he chose and then her search would be over at once.

'Some refreshment, sir, after your journey?' Jenny was asking.

It was enough to divert his attention as he agreed. Leonora hastily went back into the kitchen while Jenny and Samuel between them showed him the room they had prepared for him; for now his boxes would be placed in the old nursery next door. Leonora knew that she could not help with that. It was fainthearted but she could not bear the thought of showing him to the best room in the house, which had been her father's.

She continued, as agreed with Jenny, to prepare the light repast of cold meats and chutneys. She hoped he would like it — and the room. There were so many aspects of this situation that would be new to the others too. They had been accustomed to the Mayfield family and their ways and had hardly needed to ask what might be required at any hour of the day. Everything had run smoothly at all times. Leonora sighed. Well, they would just have to carry on as best they might and if he wanted anything done differently, he had a tongue in his head.

She had everything ready on a tray and still neither Jenny nor Samuel had returned. From the sound of voices and footsteps overhead, it seemed as if he was having a brief tour of the house already. Well, perhaps if she took it through to the dining room she could make her escape and be back in the kitchen before they came down. Would he want to eat in that big formal room on his own? Her father had always used the small family room off the kitchen. Oh, they had had such happy times in there . . . no! Stop that! She snatched up the tray and marched off with it, frowning to contain the emotion that would keep trying to bubble up.

She set it down and jumped at the cool voice behind her. 'I'll have that in the office if you please. Lucy, isn't it?'

Leonora bobbed in confusion. 'Yes, sir. Thank you. I'll take it through.'

What was he doing? Her father had never eaten in the office. Everything was turned on its heels. Somehow this small unimportant thing was upsetting her most of all.

She was shaking as she fled back to the kitchen. She could feel the colour draining from her face. 'Oh, Jenny, I can't do this, I can't watch him coming in and taking over here . . . where Father should be.'

Jenny was calm and firm. 'Yes, you can, miss — I mean, Lucy. And it won't be for long.'

Leonora took a deep breath. 'Yes, you're right. It was the shock of seeing him in our house. As if he owned it. Which he does. It was just that — I hadn't thought how I would feel. I hadn't prepared myself.'

'Come and sit down. Have a sip of cordial.'

Leonora was feeling better already. Jenny's sympathy and the chance to pause and take a breath had worked wonders. 'No, I mustn't. How would it look if he took it into his head to come into the kitchen? For a servant to be taking her ease and doing nothing? It is such a small house. He may easily take us unawares.'

Her parents had run the home on lines of easy informality, eating and relaxing in the family dining room, straight off the kitchen and coming into the domestic quarters whenever they chose, to help with any needful tasks in her mother's case, or just for a friendly chat. 'Oh, Jenny. There was so much laughter in the house when my mother was alive.'

'I know. Lucy has often said so. The best place a maid could ever have. And your father was pleasant and easy — but saddened. I could tell without Lucy telling me. But we must not harp on that, miss. We are all behind you. And why should Mr Rigton suspect anything? The truth is so out of the way that it will never occur to him.'

Leonora nodded, feeling bolder by

the minute. 'You're right. He has no reason to suspect. And as soon as he leaves the house, I must redouble my efforts and spend every waking moment I have in searching. Hopefully it will not take too long.'

'And the children will be back with you almost before you know it,' Jenny encouraged her.

'Yes, that is what I must strive for. There is no time for weakness.'

From the main office, a bell rang. Three heads switched around in apprehension. 'It's him. What on earth could he want?' Leonora's voice was barely a squeak.

'I shall go,' Samuel said firmly. 'Don't you ever go, miss, while Jenny or I can respond. I never thought to hear that old bell again. Poor Mr Mayfield just used to call. And the office door was open to the hall at all times except in the deepest winter cold. Or when he had a customer of course and needed to be private.'

'Samuel!' Jenny said swiftly with a

meaningful look at Leonora's suddenly stricken face.

'No, I am all right.' She must get a hold of herself. Obviously her father would be spoken of — and by the new master, too — and she must grow accustomed to it.

'Aye, I'm sorry,' Samuel mumbled, looking as if he might weep himself. 'I'm an old fool.' He began to shuffle to the door.

'Yes, you are,' Jenny said briskly. 'You must look sharp or he'll dismiss you in favour of someone younger. And where would Miss Leonora — I mean, Lucy — be then?'

Samuel seemed to be gone a long time. What could the new master be wanting? Leonora did her best to concentrate on the task before her but her hands would not obey her. She paused as she felt Jenny's hand on her wrist. 'You have salted that twice already.'

'Have I? I'm sorry. I'm nothing but a hindrance.'

'Of course not. He may like his pies salty. You need a little time to get used to things, that's all. You will come about, never fear.'

But she did not have time, Leonora thought. At any moment she could be discovered and sent packing. And from her brief glance at the new master she was convinced that he had a disconcertingly clever look about him. That stood to reason, for Sir Francis would hardly be employing him otherwise. He would be entirely his employer's man, from head to toe. And that therefore made him her enemy.

Samuel scurried in, almost tripping over the door sill in his panic. 'I don't know what to say. He is to be a fair new broom and no mistake.'

'Close the door,' Jenny hissed.

'What?' A glance over his shoulder. 'Ah, yes.'

'We must all be so careful now for Lucy's sake.' Jenny glared at him.

'What did he say?' Leonora pressed.

'He only wants to see all the papers.

From your father's — I mean, from Mr Mayfield's time. Going back all those years. What can he possibly want with them?'

Leonora's heart sank. 'Perhaps he means to check up on my father's work? Perhaps he and Sir Francis think that my father was inefficient — or even dishonest.'

'Well, he'll find none of that here,' Samuel said stoutly.

Leonora was thinking furiously. Since her father was dead, there could be no possible legal recourse against him. Maybe the new master thought that finding any previous irregularity would be a feather in his own cap.

No, be calm. This was foolish; his motive was obvious. Sir Francis wanted the records of her father's expenses. The amount was trifling to him but avoiding the debt was just the kind of devious practice he had always been known for. She should have thought of that before going to him, openly as she had. But for Sir Francis to avoid the debt by finding the papers first was unfair and she would not allow him to get away with it.

So it was now even more pressing that she should discover them before anyone else did.

3

Adam stared at the closed door, wishing he could hear what was being said in the kitchen. He should have felt happy, sitting in his very own office and with a secure job such as he had dreamed of but never thought he would achieve. But so far, he felt out of place and uneasy. He was trying to be stern but fair with his new servants. Friendship as such would not be fitting but he had hoped to establish a good working relationship.

Less than a month ago he had thought in despair that he would never have the opportunity to use the law qualifications Lord Northbury's generosity had paid for. The Earl, Lord Northbury, would have found him a post also, he knew, but he must make his own way. He did not want to live cap in hand on the basis of being indebted to others.

Perhaps he had answered the earl's kindness almost grudgingly, not wanting to be beholden to him and he must apologise — but his pride still held him back. When he sought another interview, he wished to show the earl what he had achieved. He must go back able to depend on his own merits and not on the basis of the boyhood friendship between the earl and Adam's father. When his parents had died and his father's debts had been repaid, Adam had had only the prospects of becoming a servant himself — a tutor at best, until Lord Northbury had offered to sponsor him. So now Adam was more than ready to treat his own servants well. If they would let him.

He smiled grimly. For one who had been so eager to avoid being answerable to a wealthier man, he half suspected that he was now doing just that — and taking on more than he had bargained for. And a strange situation also as apparently his father had been a distant cousin of Sir Francis and Adam was to be considered as heir to the Carrock estate and fortune. Sir Francis had made it plain at their first meeting, however that the succession was to be dependent on his new employer's whim. But Adam was determined to work hard and honourably and to prove himself.

Now, on his first day he seemed to be setting off on the wrong foot, though he could not understand why. A simple enough request, surely? And yet Samuel had visibly blanched when Adam had asked for Mayfield's papers. 'Ah, well, I don't quite know, sir. I expect they must be in the small office at the back of the house.' Followed by some rambling account of how Mr Mayfield had employed a clerk at times to help out but that had been some while ago and Samuel himself had had little to do with papers as such, so they could be in various places. Or perhaps the relatives had taken them, he had added hopefully, when they came to the funeral.

They took a fair few things of Mr Mayfield's with them.

Adam said patiently, 'When I say 'Mr Mayfield's papers', I mean everything that concerned his work for Sir Francis. That is what is needed. And what Sir Francis has asked for.' He frowned. He had not intended to make use of Sir Francis' authority in that way. He wanted to establish his own. But really, he did not seem to be getting anywhere.

'Perhaps one of the others — I'll just go and see.' Samuel blundered out.

'Wait a moment. Where are you going?'

Samuel's voice floated across the hall. 'To see if anyone else knows anything.' And he then remembered himself enough to return and close the door. A pity, for Adam would have been interested in hearing the result of Samuel's enquiries.

So he must wait, it seemed. No point in hounding the poor fellow. He shook his head. Perhaps, when he was settled in, he might look for someone else.

Someone who would look up to him from the start. And obviously the old man was feeling his age; with those stooped shoulders, Adam wondered that Samuel could even reach to clean the rather fine chandelier he had noticed in the dining room. He would need to entertain in there on Sir Francis' behalf and appearances must be observed. Sir Francis had made that very clear.

But he must not be too hasty. Perhaps Samuel had nowhere else to go. And Adam knew how that felt.

'Mr Rigton? Sir?' Samuel was back and looking a little more cheerful. 'Yes, that will be quite in order. But I think there are more of the kinds of thing you may be wanting in here. In that other office is where Mr Mayfield kept all the old stuff. Of little real interest and very dusty. I should begin in that cupboard by the fire if I were you.'

'Then I shall,' Adam said cordially, making a decision to investigate the other office at the earliest opportunity.

As Samuel left the room, Adam wondered if this had been a mistake. He could have made a point of asserting his authority and declared his intention to begin in that other office straightaway. He sighed. He didn't recall his own parents' household, in happier times, being so difficult.

There was a firm knock on the front door. Adam straightened his back. No doubt this would be his first matter of business. Samuel too seemed to welcome this new distraction. His steps as he crossed the hall were almost brisk. But as Samuel saw who it was, Adam heard the manservant's tone alter. And the door out into the hall was not quite shut. Adam rose and tilted his head, even more intrigued that Samuel's voice was so low. 'Why are you here?' Samuel was muttering.

The other voice was young and self-assured. 'I am about Sir Francis' business, as always. Why the long face? Come, old man, are you not going to announce me? That's what you do, isn't it? Or at least stand aside and let me in. I can announce myself.'

Adam was not having this. He flung the office door wide. Whoever this unpleasant visitor was, he must learn that Adam was not to be trifled with. 'Good afternoon. Please enter if you wish to see me.' He thought he could see at once the reason for Samuel's hesitation. The man was tall and thin, with sharp features although he was smart enough in his dress. You could never call him shabby and his coat was almost as good as Adam's own. Adam decided at once that he must get another, more in keeping with his new position, if he was to gain respect. But there was an air about the man that made Adam uneasy. And some people might have been flattered by the depth of the bow but Adam felt that it smacked of mockery.

The newcomer said, 'Sir Francis wishes to speak to you.'

'Naturally,' Adam replied. 'I was intending to visit Sir Francis at the earliest opportunity. I have only just arrived. Tomorrow morning, I thought.'

'Ah, but you see, I'm afraid that wouldn't be convenient at all. Sir Francis expressed the urgent wish to see you today — immediately, in fact.'

Adam could see that this minion was only waiting for him to show weakness by trying to argue. He had only met Sir Francis once, about a week earlier when he had first been given the news of his amazing appointment and inheritance and the arrangements had been made for his arrival. He understood only too well, however, that arguing with Sir Francis, or his commands, was not a possibility. He said pleasantly, 'Certainly. I shall order my horse at once.'

'Oh — and Sir Francis wishes to see the results of your searches. You are to bring them with you.'

'I am afraid that there at least, he will be disappointed. My searches have hardly had time to begin.'

Adam's own plan of going to Carrock Hall the following day would have made more sense. By then, he might well have found something to show to Sir Francis. But he suspected that Sir Francis knew this of course and had acted deliberately to place him at a disadvantage. This would be how he maintained his reputation and his power.

The man bowed again. 'Sir Francis will understand, I'm sure. And while you are gone, there will be no time wasted, for I am to continue here.'

'What?' Adam stared at him, unable to hide his surprise.

The man smirked. 'Tobias Henge at your service. I am to be in your employ, by Sir Francis' command. I am to have five pounds a quarter and will be your new clerk.'

★ ★ ★

Leonora, listening from the kitchen, knew that she must not be seen by this messenger from Sir Francis. From the glimpse she had across the hall as he came in, he did not seem familiar. But she could not be sure.

She accosted Samuel as soon as he re-entered the kitchen. 'Who has Sir Francis sent? Is it someone we know?'

Samuel was pulling at his collar as if unable to breathe.

'Samuel? Are you all right? Is it someone who could recognise me?'

'Recognise you? No, no — not at all. You are quite safe on that score.'

Leonora hesitated only a moment before snatching a cloth and going into the hall. She began to polish the white painted banisters. In spite of the risk, she had to know what was being said. Almost at once, her heart leapt with pleasure as she heard the man deliver his message.

Mr Rigton was to go out — already. This was what she had been waiting for but she had hardly hoped to have the opportunity so soon. As soon as her hopes were raised, however, they were once again dashed. A new clerk. Who would have thought Sir Francis would appoint one himself and so rapidly? Adam Rigton did not sound to be too pleased either. He was saying stiffly, 'I believe I would have preferred to appoint my new clerk myself.'

The sneer in the voice that replied made Leonora shiver. 'I am sorry to hear that.'

Adam said, 'I shall do as Sir Francis instructs, of course. But I trust you will give me every satisfaction in your duties. I assure you that I shall not keep you otherwise.'

'Be assured, I shall do my utmost.'

Without warning, the door opened and once again, Leonora found herself gazing straight into Adam's eyes. She knew that she should lower her head but somehow she could not. For one long moment it was as if they were locked together, neither moving. Like a rabbit caught in a hunter's trap, Leonora forgot to breathe. And yet she felt no fear. She did not know what she felt. Time seemed to have stopped.

And then one of them must have

moved slightly and the spell was broken. Perhaps it had not been so long after all. Perhaps she was imagining things.

He said, 'Ah, Lucy. Good. Are the others in the kitchen?'

'Yes.' Her voice was barely audible. 'I believe so.'

'But you are the senior maid of course and Jenny presently under your instruction. Well, I am about to introduce a new member of staff to you, it seems. To all of you.'

'Shall I bring the others out here, sir?'

'No, we shall go into the kitchen.' He smiled and his face was briefly transformed. 'I am no stranger to kitchens. And would hope not to remain a stranger to this one.'

'Yes, sir.' Leonora bobbed. 'It is your house, sir.'

'Indeed,' Adam said wryly. 'I thought it was also. But sometimes things are not as they seem.'

Owing to her eavesdropping, Leonora

knew what he meant and was almost ready to sympathise. She kept her face carefully blank, chastising herself. He was Sir Francis' man, in Sir Francis' pay and here to do Sir Francis' bidding. She must never forget that, however charmingly he smiled. If he did not like the conditions of service, that was none of her concern. He should have refused the position. She nodded and led the way, in order to give Jenny and Samuel at least a moment of warning.

Adam cleared his throat. 'I wish to introduce my new clerk, Tobias Henge. I believe Mr Mayfield employed a clerk at one time so this will not be too strange for you.' You would never believe by his manner, that he was at all disconcerted.

There was an awkward silence. Leonora felt that someone should say something — it was Samuel's place to do so, surely? But he seemed to be struck dumb. Jenny twisted her hands in her apron. 'Is he to be living in?' Glancing at Leonora as she spoke.

Of course, this was something that Lucy would ask. 'Yes,' Leonora said hastily, 'we need to know if we are to make the arrangements. Is he to be part of the household?'

The voice came from the doorway. 'Yes, indeed.'

Leonora felt her hands twitch and the others seemed startled too. None of them had heard Tobias Henge crossing the hallway. His smile of welcome was more of a leer. 'And very happy to be so, I'm sure.'

'There will be sufficient accommodation?' Adam asked.

Leonora thought swiftly. 'We have enough rooms, sir, yes. He could share with Samuel if necessary,' she said reluctantly. 'But Mr Mayfield's clerks often lived in the town. It was a very convenient arrangement.'

How on earth was she to continue with her searches now? Already she disliked the clerk. Merely standing next to him caused her skin to crawl.

'But not for me, unfortunately,' the

clerk said smoothly.

Leonora bit her lips. No one had the authority to argue. Even her father would have acquiesced if Sir Francis had taken such an idea into his head. She had to accept it. It could not be helped. And she must deal with the practicalities, since Samuel still showed no sign of doing so. 'We will have a room ready for you by this evening.'

'My box is in the yard.'

'You had best bring it in then and take it upstairs.' If he thought anyone would be waiting on him, he was to be disappointed. But it seemed he did think so for he was turning arrogantly to Samuel. As he did so, however, Mr Adam said, 'Samuel, I shall need my horse.'

'At once, sir.' Samuel glanced away so that only Leonora caught his smile of pleasure that the new clerk had been overruled. For Samuel to be concealing his feelings made sense, she reflected. No point in antagonising this other unknown who was thrust into their

51

midst. Not until they had his measure. Or even then, she reminded herself. She must not allow a petty dislike to overturn her main objective.

She said pleasantly, 'If you were to follow Samuel, he will be taking the servants' stairs down to the yard. That is the way you will be using to come in, in future. Bring your box here and I will show you the way upstairs.' She did not want him wandering around the attics at will — although eventually it would be difficult to prevent him, she supposed. But at least it might give her time to check if there were any signs of her father hiding anything there. She sighed as she waited for him. But he had managed to re-assume the oily good humour as he climbed the back stairs, box hoisted on his shoulder.

Leonora led the way and opened the first door. 'In here. Jenny or I will make up the second bed when we may.'

He glanced along the narrow corridor. 'There seem to be a lot of doors up here. Can I not have a room to myself?'

'They are mostly filled with lumber.' She thanked the stars that her words were true. If he shared with Samuel, at least there was a chance the older man could keep a watch on him — and report back.

'Which is your room?' The bold glance made her shudder.

'No business of yours,' she said sharply. He laughed, not one whit put out. She continued briskly, 'Put the box down; you can see to it later. No doubt Mr Adam will wish to inform you of your duties before he leaves.'

'No need for you to worry about that, my dear. Sir Francis himself has spoken to me at length already. My duties are clear.'

She nodded and led the way down but he paused on the first landing, looking around with interest. 'And Mr Adam sleeps on this floor?'

'Yes,' she said. In my father's room. It still pained her to think of it.

'And what are all these other rooms?'

'I cannot see that they will be of any

concern to you.' She frowned, unable to understand him. Surely Mr Adam was also Sir Francis' man through and through? And yet it seemed as if this Tobias Henge had been put here by Sir Francis to learn all he could, and about the whole household. It was almost as if he was to be a spy. Did Sir Francis not trust Mr Adam? Maybe he trusted no one. There could be another spy employed to watch Henge and yet another to watch him — and so on and so on . . .

She bit back a nervous giggle and said, 'As clerk, Mr Adam may bring you up to the drawing room on this floor when entertaining important townspeople. Or if notes need to be taken. That will be up to him. Otherwise, your domain will be the two offices downstairs. And mainly the small one at the rear of the house.'

She had looked in there, yes, but had the search been thorough enough? If only she had realised that the small office would be occupied for much of the time. If only she knew the meaning of her father's last words.

'Henge!' Mr Adam was calling from the hall.

Leonora was surprised at her feeling of relief. It was strange; she had hated the very notion of Adam's presence here but was suddenly seeing him as preferable to the odious clerk.

'The office that will be your domain is through here.' Adam gestured to the door as if he had lived at Carr House for months instead of less than a day. 'You may begin in there. I am sure it will keep you busy for the rest of the week so there will be no need for you to go elsewhere. And I will inspect what you have found before it is removed. This will be necessary if I am to perform my duties for Sir Francis efficiently.'

'I don't know about that,' Henge said sulkily.

'I intend to clarify all these discrepancies during my discussion with Sir Francis. If you have acted against his wishes in the meantime, make certain that he will know of it.'

He was only an inch taller but Adam seemed to tower over the new clerk. Leonora had to smile as the man seemed to crumple. He had been bluffing, she thought, at least in part and Adam had been observant enough to have found him out.

And at the very least perhaps the obvious enmity between the two could work to her advantage.

* * *

Adam was in no good temper as he made his return journey from Carrock Hall. Not only with his employer but with himself, as he should have expected this. The whole idea of summoning him to an interview had been nothing more than a ploy to give the odious Henge free reign to search the house; he saw that now. Adam had been kept kicking his heels in an anteroom for half an hour before being summoned to face the icy demand from

Sir Francis: why had he not provided the information needed?

Adam stared at him in disbelief. 'I have not yet had the opportunity.'

'Excuses,' Sir Francis snapped. 'You disappoint me. You will soon learn that I am not a man to be fobbed off. When I ask for something it must be produced — and produced immediately.'

Adam said nothing. He would not play Sir Francis' game. Obviously the man did not trust him and there was no reason for this. Did Sir Francis trust anyone, even Henge? Although that servant obviously thought that he did. Adam suspected that Henge would eventually be sadly disillusioned.

'You may go. If you are to realise your expectations and become my heir, I will need a better showing from you. You have made an inauspicious beginning,' Sir Francis said sourly.

Adam nodded curtly, sorely tempted to throw the man's promises back in his face. But that would be foolish. This might be merely an initial test of sorts and things might settle down.

'And you may place implicit trust in Henge. He knows my will in all things. Rely on him and you will do well.'

It struck Adam that he would be well advised to do the opposite of whatever Sir Francis suggested. No doubt he and Henge would be played off, one against the other. He said, 'I shall rely on him as he proves fit. A wise policy as you yourself have advised.'

Sir Francis glared at him, evidently displeased by this reply. 'Watch your step. Do not try to be too clever.'

'I have no intention of doing so, Sir Francis.' Adam bowed, was dismissed and withdrew.

He began to feel better as he rode and struck off into the hills, leaving the dark stone pillars and terraces of Carrock Hall behind him. A gloomy setting between the towering fells and the glass smooth lake but it was as if the house had been built only to impress.

Gradually as Adam rode his temper began to cool. He had not made too bad a showing he supposed, considering the power of his adversary. And Sir Francis was obviously well practiced at these stratagems. He was a man who could not resist controlling his subordinates by keeping them in a position of continual uncertainty. Adam's head was still buzzing with clever remarks he might have made in reply. But no doubt maintaining a dignified silence would be the wiser course; never giving away how well he understood Sir Francis and his games.

At least the friendliness he had shown the stable lad as he reclaimed his horse had borne fruit. The boy had recommended a track around the hill which would prove a good short cut and should shorten the return journey by at least half an hour. With luck, he would arrive back long before Henge was expecting him. This was the way forward.

4

Leonora was thinking furiously. The only thing to do was to combat this new challenge as best she may. At least Henge was securely in the clerk's office. She drew Samuel to one side as soon as the door had closed behind Henge and Adam's horse had disappeared from the street outside. 'I will have to continue my search at once, in the guise of cleaning the bedrooms. This will be my only chance to look in the room that was my father's.'

Samuel turned to face her, slowly, his expression strangely blank as if his thoughts were elsewhere.

'Do you understand me?' she whispered urgently. Her heart went out to the old man after all these unwelcome changes but he must be made to understand what was needed. She could not manage without him. 'As soon as Mr Adam returns, you must come and tell me immediately. Before he even enters the house. And Mr Henge too — if he begins to wander around.'

'And I'll deal with making up his bed so that you are free to get on,' Jenny said. 'But would you be better starting with Mr Adam's office? That is what we always did for Mr Mayfield, whenever he went out and we had the opportunity. Because that room was occupied so much during the day and we had to seize our chance. If we keep watch for you, you will not arouse suspicion in tackling the bedroom at any time.'

'Yes, you're quite right. I am trying to do everything at once. And we must keep a watch on Henge. I do not care for him to be alone for too long.'

Henge's voice made them all start guiltily. It was fortunate that they had all kept their voices low. Could he have overheard? He gave no sign of it. 'Any chance of a mug of something to wet my whistle? It's promising to be dry and dusty work in there.'

'Indeed not,' Jenny said sharply. 'With the day hardly begun? You must wait with the rest of us.'

Henge laughed, not seeming at all put out. 'And what have you three got your heads together about? Plots and plans, I'll be bound. Not looking to do your new master a disservice, I trust.'

Leonora said quickly, 'You may help yourself to water from the pump in the yard at any time. The water there is spring fed and good — not from the river. There are mugs on the dresser.'

'I'm glad someone here will speak to me kindly. Perhaps you will come and help me out with my labours?' Henge winked.

'I have my own labours to see to — the office and the bedrooms to clean while I have the opportunity.' She swept into the hall with her cleaning cloths, leaving Henge to the trusty Samuel. And now she must forget him for the moment. She glanced round the shelves. Where to start? Already, somehow, this office was losing the feel of her father's presence. What had her father meant? Where could he have hidden them?

She pulled at one of the heavy ledgers, coughing at the dust this brought down. No need to pretend that thorough cleaning was necessary. She hoped Mr Adam would not think this a reflection on his new servants but her father would never allow the ledgers and papers to be touched. But again — the conclusion must be the same. Where the dust was present, her father could not have concealed anything recently. She went quickly along the shelves, running her fingers across them and finding a trail of dust on each. She was hoping she would find evidence of disturbance.

No, they were all as dusty as the next. Perhaps if Henge were to search here, he could be given a duster and achieve something useful at the same time. But then — it would seem odd if she had spent time supposedly cleaning in here and left so much dust. She did her best in a short time, looked at the two ledgers her father had used most frequently and completed the day to day cleaning of dusting fireplace, sills and furniture. Her duster was filled several times and had to be shaken out at the window. This was no new task for her; she had been used to helping the servants even before their mother had died. How long ago that seemed.

If anything, she had spent most of her time helping in the warmth and happiness of the large kitchen with Robert and Sophy playing in the garden or bounding in to see what was happening, often more hindrance than help.

It had been such a happy family home. Her father's private clients from the town all knew the children well and would greet them cheerfully as Robert and Sophy scurried through the hall. No one was ever perturbed by the noise that often penetrated offices or dining room.

Now all was too quiet. She swallowed fiercely. She must not allow tears to distract her. They were all depending on her. Not only the children, for the servants were risking their livelihoods for her sake. If the deception should be discovered, heaven knew how the new master would react. Or Henge either. Nothing more certain but that word would be carried to Sir Francis by one or both and then what would happen? His influence was far reaching; he could make it difficult for the others to ever find another post if he felt inclined. And such spitefulness would be in character. Well, it must not come to that.

An hour passed more swiftly than she knew. She was hardly halfway through the shelves. She sighed, feeling disheartened. The idea had seemed so easy in the beginning when she was convinced the document would be swiftly found. She opened another book, mechanically now and rifled through the pages.

Without warning, the door was flung open.

5

Leonora stared at Adam who looked as surprised as she was. Her heart was thudding rapidly. She was certain that she looked as guilty as she felt. But no, why should she? She thought, I am Lucy. I have every reason to be here. She bobbed. 'I'm sorry, sir. I was not expecting you back so soon. I thought to give your office a good clean.'

'Most commendable, I'm sure.' Adam Rigton's voice was dry. 'But Samuel too seemed frozen in shock when I came in. Surely Mr Mayfield came and went without setting the whole household by the ears?'

'Of course. Yes. It is but that we are over-anxious to please you, sir.'

'Well, please begin by ceasing all this tiresome bobbing. You make me feel dizzy.' He put a hand to his head. 'I am sorry, Lucy. Everything is new to me, too. And Sir Francis a hard taskmaster. No doubt Mr Mayfield also found him so?'

Leonora said cautiously, 'I'm sure I don't know, sir. It isn't really my place to say.' She replaced the book.

'Do not let me interfere with your work. I merely came in to change my coat,' he said kindly.

'Oh, no — once you are in, we continue with other tasks. And now I must help in the kitchen. And see whether Jenny has finished in Samuel's room.' He was looking blank. 'So that Mr Henge may share with him.'

He sighed. 'Henge. Yes. I'm sorry his arrival was so sudden. But there will be enough room? You are accustomed to having a clerk in the house?'

'Indeed. There used to be a nursery maid for the children — who has left of course. Her room was on the first floor, next to the nursery itself. Jenny and I are to share that room, we thought. If you are agreeable. It is easier for us to be getting down to the kitchen.' And would separate them by a whole flight of stairs from Tobias Henge which was also an advantage.

'I am more than happy to leave all the domestic arrangements to you. You seem more than capable — and Jenny also.'

Leonora said briskly, 'So there is plenty of room, without our trying to clear out the attics, which would be a major task. But of course, we will if you wish. Unless you are to bring a new wife to the household?' As her father had done shortly after first being appointed, she knew. Sir Francis had at that time intimated strongly that a wife would be useful in helping to entertain his guests. Fortunately her parents were already in love and had welcomed the opportunity.

'No, no new wife as yet, I'm afraid.' Mr Rigton was smiling, seemingly amused by her question.

She reddened. Whatever had got into her? She was completely forgetting her place. It was because somehow he seemed so easy to talk to. She would have to take care; she would be betraying herself.

If he had noticed her confusion, Mr Rigton was ignoring it. 'This new position has been thrust upon me out of the blue. Only a fortnight ago, I could not have even considered keeping a wife, even if I had had anyone in mind. Even now, my position is by no means secure. I have to prove that I can please Sir Francis. Only then will he formerly announce me as his heir. Or so he has told me.'

'Oh!' She did not try to hide her surprise. 'You are related to him?'

'Very distantly. Through my father. I am a kind of cousin apparently, according to Sir Francis, though I had no knowledge of the relationship before and he had never shown an interest in me.'

'Indeed, I have got so far in my career and qualified in law through the benevolence of the Earl of Northbury, who had become our landlord. When my parents died he was kind enough to help me. But I will not ask more of him. I am determined to make my own way.' His face shadowed. 'Or I was. If it is a matter of blood I will of course fulfil my obligation to Sir Francis.'

He sighed resignedly. 'If he is to prove a difficult relative, so be it.'

'Oh, dear.' In spite of her resolutions, Leonora could not keep the sympathy from her voice.

'Yes, I am strictly on probation. If I manage the post as agent as successfully as Mr Mayfield then I may — only may — be reinforced as heir as promised. But my future is by no means certain. Sir Francis has made that abundantly clear today.'

'I see. That must be very difficult for you.'

'It is. I suppose I am no worse off than last month when I had no particular future at all. But it is hard not to be trusted. And to have one's authority belittled, with others set to spy on me.'

'You mean Henge.'

He laughed bitterly. 'Indeed I do. If ever I did not trust a man it is he. Did you ever feel an instant aversion to someone, Lucy? And yet I cannot insist he leaves purely on a dislike. It is hardly fair to the fellow, even if it were possible for me to do so.'

'No.' She was looking at him with new eyes. It seemed that nothing was as simple as she had supposed.

'I don't know why I am telling you all this. You might be just such another spy, sent here by Sir Francis who will run to him immediately to relay all my disloyal words. I am sure Sir Francis would pay you well.'

'I wouldn't do that, sir!'

He had halted in his pacing and was very near to her. 'No, I believe you would not. And as surely as I know I cannot trust Henge, I know beyond doubt that I can trust you. I do not know why.'

She was looking up at him, her duster clasped within both hands as if to create a barrier between them. Slowly her hands were falling away.

He said softly, 'You do not know how I have longed for someone to confide in. Educated poverty is a lonely state.'

And then suddenly he was kissing her.

For a moment Leonora could hardly believe what was happening. She was frozen with surprise, before her thoughts melted into a confusion of feeling as she returned his kiss. With no thought for commonsense or her task she gave a little murmur of pleasure and he jerked away, so suddenly that she swayed back against the bookshelves.

He said, 'What must you think of me? I am not the kind of man to take advantage of a maidservant. It is against every principle I have ever held.' He groaned. 'What have you done to me, Lucy?'

Leonora said, 'I must go and help Jenny,' and fled from the room.

6

Leonora knew that she should feel angry. She did, didn't she? As he had said himself, he had no right to take such a liberty. And yet these things happened all the time to those who were employed in service. But he had apologised at once. It was unlikely to happen again.

She clung onto the end of the banister rail, surprised by the strength of her feelings. She was almost overwhelmed by her sense of loss. She had not shrunk from his kiss; she had welcomed it. Oh, if only she were not in this horrible situation. If only she had been introduced to him as Leonora and still had fond parents to arrange matters.

But she had not and if she did not apply herself, would have to take a position as governess or companion and become old without ever meeting anyone who would love her, let alone take on the children. She would spend the rest of her life thankful for being fed and housed. No, that must not happen. Nothing and no one must distract her from her aim.

Samuel came from the kitchen, his face flustered. 'Miss — er — Lucy. I'm sorry. I didn't know . . . '

'Yes!' Leonora's confusion made her sharper than she had intended. 'Where were you? You were going to warn me.'

He lowered his voice. 'I didn't know he had returned. I was detained . . . '

'Warn you of what, Miss Lucy? And we are very polite all of a sudden are we not?' Tobias Henge slid from his office doorway where he had obviously heard every word.

It was fortunate that they had said nothing too incriminating. Leonora said quickly, 'I was cleaning in the master's office. Naturally I did not wish to be there when he returned, needing to use the room. That is never done, not in a

74

well-run household.' She took a deep breath to calm herself. 'And I do not need to justify myself to you.'

He gave one of his mocking bows. 'And yet you have and very charmingly too. Surely the household may only run well if we all know what the others are doing and may work together and in accord?'

'On the contrary, we all need to know our own duties and perform them as best we may. That will be quite sufficient. But if you feel that you do need assistance in gathering the papers together for Sir Francis, we may well be able to help you.'

Henge looked less certain. 'I'm sure that won't be necessary.'

Leonora seized the opportunity and swept past him into the small room. Her eyes widened in angry surprise. Piles of papers were strewn everywhere, even some on the floor. She said, 'This is intolerable. This office is a mess. It was never kept so in my — Mr Mayfield's time. Well, whether you wish my assistance or not, you are going to have it. I thought you were merely looking through to see what was here. It seems to me that you have been searching for something in particular.'

Henge's voice was sullen. 'Only to see if there might be something of interest to Sir Francis.'

'No,' Samuel said suddenly, with a worried look. 'Tobias has not been doing anything untoward. I have been watching him, I assure you.'

Why was Samuel defending the odious man? Leonora said firmly, 'I shall supervise now and assist you in replacing what is not needed. And what Sir Francis does want will hardly benefit from being flung onto the floor.'

'Do not interfere.' Henge snatched a pile of papers away from her. 'This is the clerk's sanctum. Nothing to do with you.'

'The tidiness and upkeep of the house is very much to do with me!' She welcomed the conflict and having somewhere to direct her anger. And it was time they stood up to him.

'What is going on here?'

They all stopped as Adam Rigton came into the room. There was no need to protest about what had happened, Leonora thought. The keen eyes were taking everything in at a glance. With a frown, Adam was saying, 'Your searches seem to have been over-enthusiastic, Henge. I certainly think you need someone to assist you in replacing everything. In fact, I will do so myself. And at the same time, you will tell me what you have found that is of interest to Sir Francis. Obviously if I am to fulfil my duties efficiently, I shall need to know what has gone before and will need to discuss these matters with my employer.'

'It will be dusty work.' Leonora was reluctant to lose her opportunity.

'I think Henge and I will cope with a little dust. Thank you, Lucy.'

She was dismissed. Henge gave her a look that was a mixture of triumph and hatred. He would resent being reprimanded in front of her and Samuel. She looked him straight in the eye as she left the room, not wanting him to think she was afraid of him. As she entered the kitchen, her heart was thudding. Samuel's voice was soft and regretful as he followed her. 'Be careful, miss. You have made an enemy there, I fear.'

Yes. In less than half an hour she had made an enemy of one person and something altogether more of another. Suddenly, everything in her life was becoming very complicated.

The more she thought about the events of the day, the less she understood her feelings. When Samuel came to apologise to her yet again, she could hardly remember what he was talking about.

'I neglected to warn you. I am so sorry . . . '

'Warn me?' Leonora said stupidly. She was thinking of the way Adam had pressed his lips against hers and his strong arms around her.

'You see, Tobias distracted me. That's how he is. Ties you in knots with his clever words. Mr Adam was in the house and past me so quickly. But it was all right, Miss Leonora, wasn't it? He did not seem angered.'

'All right?' Leonora realised there was a desperate need for reassurance in the old man's face. 'Oh, yes.' She hardly knew what she was saying.

'He didn't find out what you were doing in there? Your secret is safe?'

'My . . . ? Oh. Of course. No, he has no idea.'

'I will be more careful next time. It will not happen again, I promise you.'

'I am sure it will not.' Leonora did not know whether that was what she wanted or not. But what was she thinking of? Of course it was not what she wanted. Adam was her father's supplanter, Sir Francis' man and as such, could never be regarded as anything but an enemy.

The days passed. She entered into a

routine, helped by Jenny and Samuel, of avoiding both Adam and Tobias Henge and getting on with her search. The men were both busy with their own concerns and duties and now that Adam was beginning to take up the reins in full, he was out for much of the time — visiting prospective voters in the town. And taking Henge with him whenever he could devise a reason. Or so Leonora thought. He seemed as little inclined to leave Tobias Henge in the house unattended as Leonora was herself.

★ ★ ★

'It is my belief that Henge is stealing from the kitchen,' Jenny muttered. 'The entire seed cake I made yesterday has gone — and even some of the suet pudding.'

'Surely not! How long has this been going on?' Leonora asked.

'Only the last couple of days or so. But enough is enough. The gaps are always tidied around and hidden with extra scallions or lettuce so I hardly noticed at first. But now I'm looking out for it and it's happening more often.'

'I suppose he's entitled to his food,' Leonora said.

'Meals, yes. But not in this sneaking way — and spoiling dishes intended for the master or even his guests.'

Leonora frowned. Why would Henge do that? Maybe he was trying to cause trouble for Adam. Guests might report back to Sir Francis that they had been ill-fed at his agent's house. But it would not only be Adam who would take the blame. 'It will reflect on us, if so. Have you tackled him?'

As if on cue, Tobias Henge grinned around the doorway and slid into the kitchen. 'I smell something cooking I believe. And tasty too.'

'I'll thank you to wait until your portion is served to you,' Jenny snapped.

Tobias Henge seemed pained. 'As if

I'd do anything other.' His face gleamed with what they were certain was a secret amusement.

'No one helps themselves before time. Or takes from plates intended for the dining room. Not in my kitchen.'

'Why, has someone been doing that, pretty Jenny? Not I, I can assure you,' Tobias Henge laughed.

'Well, keep out of here until the food is ready,' Jenny said. 'Could you get some vegetables and salads, please, Lucy? We will need more now.'

Leonora smiled grimly as she went down the stairs leading to the scullery and then the garden. The exchange had seemed good humoured enough in a way but they must never forget the threat that Tobias Henge posed.

She opened the heavy door out into the small back yard area and stopped. Surely there had been a flash of movement in one of the outbuildings? Too swift to be the gardener, who was even older than Samuel and besides this was not his day for working here. Had she imagined it? Should she go and tell Samuel? But asking for help would have to mean that Henge would be sticking his nose in. She would rather manage alone. It was probably only one of the village children after the ripening fruit — little scamps. Though when that happened, they usually scaled the garden wall at the back and made off along the river bank.

The outbuildings were few and small; it would not take long. She moved softly to look inside the first door. Nothing in the shadows here. And nowhere to hide among the tools — scythe, spades, rakes. On impulse, she helped herself to a rake and held it before her. You never knew, although she must present a pretty picture indeed. Next the stable, as they had always called it — hardly more than a single stall, land being scarce in town. Her father had kept a horse at times but had decided eventually to leave the animal at Town End farm — and this was what Adam had chosen to do also.

At first she thought this to be empty too. The straw did not seem to be heaped enough to conceal anyone. She held her breath. No, it was indeed empty. About to turn and leave, she heard a muffled sneeze.

'Come out at once,' she shouted, without thinking. 'I know you are there.' She glanced behind her, looking up at the house. For once, the lurking Tobias might have been useful but there was no sign of anyone. She held the rake in front of her. 'I warn you!' She jabbed at the straw a little, just enough to disturb, not to do damage.

The straw rose with a screech. 'Don't hurt me. It's me, Leo.'

She stopped, rake aloft, with her mouth open. 'Robert! But you are in Penrith with Cousin Talbot.'

The boy shook the straw from his shoulders, recovering a little of his dignity. 'I hated it there. I'm running away to sea,' he said defiantly.

'You silly child!' No, best not to hurt his feelings, however foolishly he had behaved. She said cautiously, 'But we are five miles and more from the sea here, Robert.'

'I know that. But I had to pass here anyway. I'm collecting provisions.'

'Oh, so it was you who took the food.' Now she understood.

'I am staying here until I have filled my sack and then I will stow away. Cousin Talbot laughed at me and said I was too young and that no one would take me without payment. So I thought at first I would ask you if you had any money and then I knew you had not. So I decided I am going to get on board and hide, eating some of my food and then creep out when no one is about and show them how useful I can be. I shall look for unfinished tasks and complete them. Like the boggarts and elves do, in the old tales, helping in the night. And then the captain will keep me on.'

'Oh, Robert.'

'You see, I am not being foolish. I have it all worked out.'

'I see that you have.' She was thinking furiously. How could she have forgotten Robert's burning ambition? 'But when we receive the money owed to us, we can get you signed on properly as a midshipman, rather than one of the hands.' Was that how it was done? She would have to find out.

'But you have been looking for the money for weeks. And I'm not staying at Cousin Talbot's any more.'

Her quest had never seemed so hopeless. She knew that mutinous look.

'Don't try to send me back, Leo. I shall only run away again.'

'I know. I shan't, I promise.' She twisted her hair in her fingers.

'And what are you doing here anyhow? Cousin Talbot wouldn't tell me where you were. He said you were ungrateful and that he didn't know and didn't care anyway.'

'I'm sure he did. But this is a secret, Robert. You must promise me that you will not tell anyone.'

'No, of course not. I am a secret

myself. I only came here for food and to ask Samuel where you were and then I could find you and see about the money.' He shook his head. 'I never thought it would take so long, Leo.'

'Ssh, I have to think. You can't stay here.'

'Why not? I can hide whenever I hear someone coming. Like I did when you came, Leo.'

'We have a new clerk,' Leonora explained quickly. 'He is called Mr Henge. You must not, on any account, let him see you, or even suspect that you are here. He is not to be trusted. He would go straight to Sir Francis — or think of something even worse to do. And of course, Mr Adam must never see you either.'

'Or he will go straight to Sir Francis too. I understand.'

Leonora paused. 'I'm not sure about him. But it is not a risk I intend to take. I will hide you upstairs somehow, where I will be better able to protect you. Wait here. Hide under the straw again, for now, and do not come out until you hear my voice call your name. I will go and make sure it is safe.'

She ran into the house to find Samuel. 'Has Mr Adam called for his horse, or is he out on foot?' She tried to think; how long had he been gone? Her father had always had certain days when the tenants would find him at home and days when he was out collecting rents — but so far, Adam had been much less predictable. If only he would get into a routine . . .

Samuel was grimacing and shaking his head. What could he mean? 'Are you trying to tell me you don't know?' She could scream in frustration.

A familiar sneering tone came from behind her. 'You seem mighty interested in the master's movements for a maidservant. And one who isn't even to be here for much longer. That Jenny must be a slow learner — but then, I can't say I see you trying to teach her anything much.'

She snapped, 'You see to your work,

Tobias Henge, and I will attend to mine!' She turned to the stairs and walked up with a slow dignity, resisting the aching temptation to run, knowing that he was watching her. As she reached the top, the doorbell jangled. She could hear Samuel opening it; his voice seemed unusually loud. Was that for her benefit? 'Mr Rigton is not at home, sir, but his clerk, Mr Henge is here. I am sure he will answer your query.'

She smiled. Well done, Samuel. She fled into what had been the nurse's room. Small and unused and only reached through the one-time children's room where she and Jenny were now sleeping. Robert's presence could easily be concealed in this small space for a short time. Henge had no reason to come here and after his initial inspection of the house, Mr Adam had never ventured into these rooms. Why would he?

A tap at the door made her heart leap. Had Henge followed her after all?

But it was only Samuel. 'Just wanted to tell you, miss. I made sure to show Mr Grantham into the clerk's office and Henge will be occupied for some time because once Mr Grantham gets started he forgets why he's come and how to finish.'

Leonora smiled. 'Oh, bless you, Samuel. That's wonderful.'

'So whatever you're doing, I reckon he'll be out of the way for at least a good half hour.'

'Thank you. You see, what has happened is . . . '

He held up a hand. 'No, please don't tell me. The thing is — I'm getting old, I know it, and what I don't know can't be let out by mistake.'

'But Samuel, you would not. I have faith in you and your loyalty.'

'No, miss.' His face was clouded. 'There is more to it.'

She waited, thinking he was about to say something else. But he shook his head. 'What am I doing? Wasting the valuable time we have gained. Quick, miss and I will keep guard on the office, downstairs.'

He was gone, surprisingly swift for one of his years.

No time to wonder what he had been trying to tell her. She took up a pile of linen — just in case Henge should see her — and went quickly but silently down. Jenny was in the kitchen and Leonora quickly whispered to her what she had found and what was intended. Jenny needed no long and needless explanations. 'I didn't think the poor lad would stay there long. Not from what I saw of those relatives of yours — and have heard in the village. And of course I will help — in any way I may.'

Back now to Robert and to impress upon him the need for silence. This was not a problem now as he was throwing himself into what was almost a game with enthusiasm. She said, 'And you must keep to that as long as you are in the house. A midshipman — or any seaman — must learn to follow orders. That is the first requirement.'

'Yes.' He nodded solemnly. 'I understand. And when I am a Captain I will give the orders.'

'Even a Captain must take orders from his superiors. Commodores and Admirals and suchlike.'

'I suppose so.' His face brightened. 'I expect I will be an admiral then.'

'I am sure you shall. But first you must be a very silent stowaway in nurse's old room.' She left him there, wondering on the wisdom of this. It must not be for long. A lively noisy boy could not contain his energies indefinitely. She could hardly expect him to.

She smiled to herself, hearing the voices issuing from the office. Henge was saying, 'But I can't help you with that.'

'Yes, most unfortunate and if only I could have set out earlier I should have caught Mr Rigton myself. But my wife would delay me with some foolish matter of being displeased with our cook — as if that should be my domain, I ask you. Yes, I wish I had caught Mr

Rigton and as soon as I see him, I shall be telling him face to face. No doubt about that.'

'There is little need to tell me then.'

But old Grantham ignored the rudeness of the reply if he noticed it at all and was off again. Adam was in for a treat, Leonora thought. She whipped into the kitchen. 'All well?' Jenny mouthed.

'Yes, for now.'

'I've got Robert something to eat — here.'

'Oh, well thought of. That will keep him quiet for a while. But I suspect he already has a store of all the food gone missing from the kitchen over the last day or so.'

Jenny chuckled. 'I'd already thought of that. But the false accusations wouldn't hurt Tobias Henge. He'll be used to them, I'm sure, with that unpleasant manner of his. And he will have had many not so false in his time, no doubt of that. But see, I have wrapped a piece of pie and an apple and some cheese, and some fresh baked bread. And when you are certain you are not observed, there is a jug of fruit cordial.'

'We should make him eat what he took first, I cannot condone it.'

'He hasn't still got them? Did he not eat them straight off?' Jenny shook her head. 'I thought Master Robert had a good appetite.'

Leonora laughed. 'His provisions for the voyage apparently. But I must look in his bag — it will be a mess of crumbs and fit for nothing if I know him.' She went out into the hall and paused for a moment as old Mr Grantham's voice seemed to be nearing the short corridor leading to the clerk's office. Was the visitor about to leave? But all was well, the voice receded. He must be pacing up and down as he spoke. She turned and sped up the stairs unseen.

Robert welcomed the pie avidly but after the first couple of mouthfuls, he hesitated, looking at the brown leather bag on the floor beside him and which he had clutched as they came into the house. 'I've had enough now. I'll save the rest.'

'No. You need to eat. And dear child, do you think we would send you to sea unprepared? Everything you need will be found for you.' Somehow or other. She was determined on that. 'But by the time you set sail, the food you have there will be spoiled. And it was stealing you know — this is no longer our house and the food here is provided by Mr Rigton.'

'Oh. I didn't think of that. I'm sorry then.' He paused, frowning. 'But you're still here.'

She sighed. 'I'm working here, for the moment. Not for long.' She reached for the bag.

Robert snatched it away and delved inside himself, obviously not willing to part with his precious hoard. 'I found something, Leo. Out in the stall.'

She smiled, shaking her head. 'If you are thinking to distract me . . . ' She stopped, staring at the leather pouch he was holding out. The pouch that her father had used to carry documents. She said, 'Have you looked inside?' She wanted to laugh and dance. For surely — and after all that searching inside the house. She was hardly daring to hope. But it must be.

He said, 'It's papers. And in father's writing.'

'Let me see.' She opened the pouch and took them out. Several pages and the top one was just as she had expected. Yes, this was indeed the proof of their claim. And if Robert had not hidden himself in the stall . . . 'Oh, Robert, I could hug you. This is the answer to everything.' She turned the pages and froze as something else caught her attention.

The colour drained from her face and she could hardly believe what she was seeing.

7

Adam had resolved to keep his temper but these interviews with Sir Francis were becoming ever more trying. Deliberately so, no doubt.

Sir Francis leaned back in his chair, seemingly bored. 'I have had adverse reports of your servants. I am surprised that you have been willing to take on another man's staff.'

'I saw no reason to do otherwise. The household seems to be functioning adequately. More than adequately. And these servants know your tenants and what they expect and provide it in every way.'

'Any half decent servant will do the same. No, they are laughing at you behind your back. Concealing things. Muttering in corners. I care not a jot for you obviously but in ridiculing you they pour scorn on your position and therefore on me.'

No need to wonder where this information had come from. Adam said, 'Henge is mistaken. I suspect him to be a mischief maker working to advance his own ends.'

'I have employed him and I trust him. Have a care in your remarks.' Sir Francis paused. 'Yes. I have decided what you must do. You will sack the lot of them and employ new. Immediately.'

Adam rocked on his heels. 'But there is no fair cause. And they will have to be given notice.'

'Have to? I think not. I am in control here,' Sir Francis said sharply. 'What I command is what happens.'

Adam struggled to control his anger. That would help no one. 'I cannot agree with this.' He clenched his fists. He could not do it. What would become of Lucy?

'Your agreement is of no importance.' Sir Francis gave an almost imperceptible nod and Adam found his arms were grasped and none too gently, by two large footmen as he was escorted to the door.

As he rode away Adam was thinking hard. There was nothing he could do to help the three servants stay on if Sir Francis had ordained that they must go. And without the income he received from Sir Francis he could not afford to pay them himself. But he did not intend to let the injustice go unchecked. He must make certain that they received excellent references from himself. He could even help them to find other posts — Lord Northbury might be able to assist there — although such positions might be some distance away. And no bad thing, in one respect, that all of them — and Lucy in particular-should be out of reach of Sir Francis and his tyrannical empire.

But even so, to have Lucy so far away. Would he ever see her again? His heart was sore at the thought of it. I cannot do it, he thought — I love her! The realisation brought a great lightening in the whole of his being. A truth that had been there all the time, only waiting for him to catch up with himself and recognise it.

He covered a mile with his anger tempered with flashes of delight before he began to think what must be done next. He must protect her somehow. As his wife she would be safe of course, but he was in no position to support a wife. Not as yet — and even so, it all depended on whether she would have him. But surely she must. She had responded to his ill-timed kiss, he was certain of that.

But what had he to offer her? And how would Sir Francis respond to the thwarting of his command? He did not care. Just as long as she had nothing to do with Tobias Henge and was well away from him.

As he came away from the shadow of the hill to join the main road, he knew what he would do.

He would give up all thought of the inheritance, for he never believed it certain. And Sir Francis can make

Henge his heir if he is so fond of him, for all he cared. He smiled grimly. Yes, he would set up his own lawyer's practice — in London or somewhere. As he had always intended before receiving Sir Francis' surprising summons. He would be no worse off. Indeed, a great deal better. He would have the love of his life by his side and the freedom to do as he wished. None of this slinking about, trying to please a man who did not deserve such subservience.

The decision made, he knew he must act at once. For further haste, he handed his horse in at the adjacent farm and was pleased that a lad came out at once to take him. He gave the animal a grateful pat on the sweating neck for he had ridden him hard while he played out his frustration and anger. The horse pricked his ears and whickered as if he had understood the need for haste and forgave it.

But in one way at least Adam knew he must be cautious. He would allow

Henge to witness him supposedly following the command and announcing the decision to the servants. Henge would report it back as no doubt he did with everything. But Adam would not play with Lucy's feelings; that would be too cruel. First, he would tell her of his love for her so she would know that her future at least was assured. And for that, Henge must be out of the way. Adam must think of some errand perhaps.

As it happened, Henge fell into his hands. 'I have had an interminable morning with Grantham,' he grumbled. 'And he must come again and tell it all to you. He simply wouldn't listen when I tried to tell him so. I'll not have this. You must speak to him.'

Adam raised his eyebrows. 'Must I? Why not complain of him to Sir Francis? Try it. Because unfortunately for you, Sir Francis needs his support. And his vote. As he needs the support of certain other gentlemen. But I am not going to discuss your complaints at present. I need you to deliver a note for me.' He thought quickly, inspired by Henge's uncomfortable experience. Ah yes, he would make it a note to someone who lived at the other end of town and talked at length, even more than Mr Grantham. Yes, he had it. The very person. 'And wait for the reply if you please.'

'I am not a messenger boy. Why not give a coin to any lad in the street?'

'And I will tell Sir Francis you entrust his business to the town's children.'

Still grumbling, Tobias Henge departed. It had not been difficult for Adam to scribble a swift letter sounding as if it was of the greatest importance without going into many details. If Henge read it, he would be no wiser — and yet the need for Adam to maintain friendly contact and speak with the various voters in the town was sound. At last Henge was off the premises and Adam could follow his heart.

'Where is Lucy?' he demanded of

Samuel. But he could see at once that she was not in the kitchen or the other rooms on this floor. No time to waste to listen to Samuel's mumbled reply. Upstairs then and he must hurry as there was no knowing how long Tobias Henge would be. Reluctant to go, he would make all speed to come back, Adam was sure.

He ran swiftly but silently up the stairs; he had a sudden boyish impulse to surprise her at her everlasting dusting, to seize her in his arms and to feel her soft lips surrender to his once more. No, she was not in the main room — but there were slight sounds coming from across the corridor. And he knew Samuel and Jenny were both downstairs so here she was. He passed through the room where the female servants now slept — seeking to avoid Henge as much as possible he suspected and who could blame them? And this was, yes, the room where the nurse had been. But at the door he paused, frowning. Yes, there were voices inside. Lucy must be talking to someone — but who?

He pushed the door open and was upon them, not knowing what he expected — but not what he saw.

Lucy was standing facing him, one hand extended in front of a small boy as if to protect him. The other hand was clasping a sheaf of papers to her breast. But it was her face that confounded him. She was staring at Adam with an expression little short of terror. All the colour had drained from her cheeks and her face was like whey. Abruptly she whipped the papers behind her back, as if hoping he had not noticed them.

He felt a sharp pain, knowing that somehow he had caused that fear and horror and when he loved her so much, wanting nothing else but to protect her. His voice, caused by the anguish of the realisation, was sharper than he intended. 'Who is this? What is he doing here?'

The boy seemed the only one of the

trio not out of countenance. He said, 'I am Robert Mayfield and I will not be staying here long. I am to go to sea.'

Adam knew at once. Lucy's protectiveness of the boy — and the unmistakable resemblance. They had the same dark curls and grey eyes. A great many things were suddenly clear. But he said only, 'I am pleased to make your acquaintance, Master Mayfield. May I wish you well in your endeavour. If you will permit me — I should like to speak to your sister alone. And if you go into my room and look in the second drawer of the small cabinet, I believe you may find something of great interest to you. Something that has undergone a sea voyage itself.'

Robert smiled. 'Ah, a guessing game. I shall bring it straight back.'

'No, once you have found it, you will sit on the small chair by the window and eat it. Slowly, mind.'

Robert laughed and was gone in an instant. Adam wanted only to take this enchanting girl in his arms but he could see that she was still wary. Did she think he would be angry to find her brother here? 'Do not worry about Robert's presence. He seems a promising lad. I am sure we shall be able to deal with him suitably.'

She gasped and stepped backwards. Whatever had he said to bring about such a reaction?

He blundered on. 'Please, I only want to help you, both of you. I would like nothing better than to have the right to protect you for the rest of my life.' This was not the way he had imagined it but there was so little time to show her his true feelings and good intentions. 'Lucy, will you be my wife?'

'Why?' she demanded.

It was hardly the reaction he had hoped for. 'Because it is the best way. Sir Francis has commanded that I must have new servants and as my wife you would be protected and honourably. I can provide for you and the rest of your family. Even if it means breaking with Sir Francis myself. We could move to live somewhere else and I could set up as a lawyer. Times might be hard at first until I am established but I am sure that — '

Now she was angry. 'How could you think . . . ?' Her voice was low and furious. 'But you see, I know now. You mock me, sir. Seizing on my regrettable moment of weakness.'

He shook his head. 'But I am offering marriage. I have never been more serious. I love you.'

'That is easy for you to say.' Her fist went to her mouth.

'Give it some thought, please. Because where else can you go?'

She turned away, staring out of the window, as if fighting some inner battle. 'All right. I will consider your offer. If my brother can stay here tonight, then I will give you my answer in the morning,' she replied.

He had to be content with that. For now. But whatever her answer and for whatever reason, he was not going to allow her to leave here without his help and protection. He was determined on that.

He left the room and Leonora stared again at the papers she had been holding behind her back. The first sheet was as she had always expected, and detailed the expenses her father had been owed by Sir Francis. Four thousand pounds. More than enough to fulfil her plans. It was everything she had hoped for.

But the other. How long had her father known about this? He had never spoken about his parents. Leonora had never thought to ask. And now she could hardly believe the evidence she was holding in her shaking hands. She whispered the words to make them seem more real 'My father was Sir Francis Carrock's heir. No — I have it wrong. My father should have been in Sir Francis' place from the start, instead of him. Sir Francis' father had actually married twice — and first and secretly to a lady who must have been my grandmother.'

Her first instinct had been to think how wonderful this was. There would be no need to worry about money ever again. They would all three be provided for.

Robert ran into the room, his sticky face glowing. 'He's gone, hasn't he? And I wanted to thank him. See, he gave me an orange. And I have saved you a piece.'

'No, it's all right. You have it.' She stared at Robert. Was this why their father had died? Why he had been murdered? Because he had discovered his rights — and made the fatal mistake of telling Sir Francis of them?

And now Robert also was in great danger. Certainly from Sir Francis and anyone loyal to him. And Adam? Her heart dropped. She felt cold with grief. Adam's position and inheritance were at risk from Robert's existence. But he had seemed a good man. She realised that she had been on the brink of losing her heart to him. And how she wished she could accept his proposal. But she must now consider what must lie behind it. What easier way to ensure that he had Robert in his power and safeguard his own future? And his talk of leaving Sir Francis and setting up on his own would be merely a ploy to allay her suspicions.

She realised now why Robert had found the papers hidden in the stable. She swallowed back ready tears. Her father must have intended taking them with him to confront Sir Francis and at the last minute thought better of it. He had pushed them into a gap in the stones intending to retrieve them later when he returned.

And he never did return. Or at least barely alive, able only to whisper a message she had not understood. She slapped a fist with frustration. She should have realised all of this. Her father had tried to warn her and she had done the worst thing possible in staying here. She should have taken the position with Aunt Merridew's elderly relative, far away from Sir Francis.

Somehow she should have stayed more aware of what was happening to Robert and insisted he should be better treated. Perhaps then he too would have agreed to stay where he was.

Robert was wiping his fingers on his shirt, smiling blissfully. 'I'm glad I came back. And when you tell Mr Adam you'll marry him, he will find me a ship and everything will be all right.'

'Robert! Our conversation was private.'

'I know. That is why Mr Adam sent me to look for the orange. But father's old room is only the other side of this wall and if you open the wardrobe you can always hear what is said in here. You know that, Leo, from playing hide and seek.'

'I had forgotten,' Leonora said distractedly. 'But Robert — I have not told Mr Adam that I will marry him.'

'But you will, won't you? And then everything will be all right anyway.'

'No.'

'But you told him you would think about it.'

'To give us time.'

He frowned. 'Why do we need time?'

'To run away. To hide. Listen, I cannot explain fully. There are a lot of things you cannot understand.'

'That is what grown-ups always say.'

'You must trust me about this.' Should she tell him of his danger? She dismissed that almost at once. She did not want to frighten him. And there was the possibility that he might confide in the most unlikely and unsuitable people. Better that he should know nothing.

'Well, I think you are being stupid, Leo. Just when we find someone who can help me do what I have always wanted, you say we have to run off.'

'You will understand one day, I promise.' She knew how feeble that sounded. And if Robert only knew just how much part of her was treacherously urging her common sense to let all caution fly and accept Adam's proposal.

He said, 'I could understand now if

you would tell me.'

She shook her head. 'I cannot. It will be for the best. Truly.'

Jenny appeared at the door. 'Master Adam wants to speak to us — right away. He looks as grim as a clogged chimney.'

Leonora took a deep breath. 'Yes. I believe I know what this is about.'

'You do? Is it going to be all right?' Jenny asked.

'I am afraid not.' Leonora turned to Robert. 'Now, I will not be long. Stay here quietly and in a few hours only, we will be on our way.'

'Where to?' Robert demanded.

'To begin with, I think we may be able to seek refuge with the real Lucy and her new husband. I am certain they will be willing to help us.'

Robert glowered. 'But John Hesket is a farmer. And they live over towards Keswick somewhere. That's entirely the wrong way.'

'Not for long. And it will be for the best.'

'Miss — you must come.' Jenny's voice was urgent.

'Yes.' They hurried down the stairs. Mr Adam was waiting in the hall, his face shadowed. 'I will speak to you all here in my office. Samuel is arrived already.' He ushered them inside and began to close the door. But Henge was insinuating his narrow face through the gap.

'Do you not want me present?' He was sneering; it was obvious to Leonora that he knew what this was about and was gloating over the downfall of his fellows.

'Your company will not be required. As you are employed directly by Sir Francis, this will not apply to you,' Adam said firmly. He closed the door and turned to face the three of them.

Even though she guessed what Adam was about to say, Leonora's heart was thudding.

'I wish you to know that this is by no desire of mine. I am apparently to begin again in my position here with an entirely new household of servants.'

Jenny gasped, her hand to her mouth.

Samuel was nodding. 'That's all right, sir. No less than we expected from the start. We were surprised to be kept on.'

'This does not reflect on your work. I have been thoroughly satisfied with all of you. And will make sure you have excellent references which will explain the circumstances.'

'That is very good of you, sir,' Jenny said, obviously recovering from the first shock of the announcement. 'And Samuel is right. We always knew. How long do we have?'

'I shall certainly not turn you out into the street, whatever instructions may arrive from Sir Francis. But if you could make some alternative arrangement as soon as possible?'

'And I have various clients to see within the next day or so. I could make enquiries with them if you wish.'

'Don't you trouble, sir. That isn't usual. It would be welcome if we could find something temporary but it's not that long to the next hiring fair, not really. We shall manage.'

'I do not care for what is usual. I wish only to do what is right.'

'Pardon me, sir but it will help none of us if you endanger your own position by going against Sir Francis,' Jenny observed shrewdly.

'Aye,' Samuel said. 'We've witnessed many such interferences on his part. Once he has spoken, there's no gainsaying him. He'll have his finger in every pie, however small.'

The two girls paused in the hall for a moment as they left the room, exchanging glances. 'Lucky you have other arrangements in mind,' Jenny murmured to Leonora.

'Yes.' Leonora tapped Jenny's arm to signal caution for here was Tobias Henge again, sliding in through the back stairs but with an unpleasant smile in their direction until he was once more in the clerk's office.

'And where's he been skulking off to

now?' Jenny muttered. 'Round to the front to listen at the window, I'll be bound. It didn't suit that he wasn't allowed to witness our discomfort. He's someone I shan't be sorry to see the last of.'

Leonora nodded. 'I had hoped to let Lucy know we were coming. Do you think she will mind if Robert and I arrive unannounced?'

'Of course not. She said she would do anything to help. I may end up there myself if I have to make my way back to mother in Keswick. But I hope to find something else here.'

'I hope you will. If it was only up to me — but I have no say in anything now.' Leonora felt near to tears.

'Oh, come, Miss Leonora, it's not like you to be down at heart. Depend upon it, you will retrieve your fortunes. You are so pretty and obviously a lady — some rich gentleman will see your true qualities and marry you and all your troubles will be over.'

Leonora tried to smile through the

arrow of pain that took her by surprise. She did not want Jenny's 'rich gentleman'. She wanted only Adam. But that was not possible when she did not know whether she could trust him. That was a risk she dare not take.

It was best not to think about that. And there were things to do, if she and Robert were to make their escape before Adam came seeking her for her answer. She must be practical.

Henge came out of the office with his coat on; she paused for a moment, not wanting him to see where she was going but for once, he was about his own concerns and showed no interest.

She went briskly up the stairs. Robert's packing was done, she supposed, but she must see how much she could usefully carry. She would do that first. Talking to Robert would only distract her when he was so disappointed. He would be sure to be arguing again, unable to accept that they were to set off in the wrong direction.

Fortunately she had been prepared for this; knowing that at any time Adam or Henge might discover her deception and that she might have to leave in a hurry, she had packed a small bundle accordingly. Taking care as she gathered things together that she must look like a maidservant in between work as she travelled. And perhaps Robert might carry something more. A pity that all his useful clothing was left behind at Penrith but that could not be helped.

It did not take long. She had worked quickly and quietly to avoid Robert interrupting her and now she opened the adjoining door, thinking he might have fallen asleep. This was the first true warmth and comfort he had known in several days. But he was very quiet. Too quiet, she realised suddenly with a plunging feeling beneath her breastbone. And the room was empty.

Foolishly, she stared from ceiling to window before bending to look under the bed. But there was nowhere he could hide himself. She said aloud, 'He cannot have left the house.' Knowing as she spoke that this was exactly what he could have done. The privacy that the closed door of the office had given them against Tobias Henge, which she had fully approved, must have given Robert the means to leave unseen.

But she must not assume he had left the house altogether. He could be in any of the other rooms — might have decided to collect some boyish treasure he had left behind. He himself had mentioned their games of hide and seek. He might even have thought that if he hid himself thoroughly enough she might leave without him.

She hurried upstairs to the attics — the younger children had always loved playing up there in the unused rooms below the roof. But the cluttered rooms were empty, no sign of eager footprints in the dust. She raced down again, hardly caring that her steps must be audible throughout the house. After his announcement, Mr Adam would expect his servants to be in turmoil, making hurried preparations for their departure.

A quick glance into the formal drawing room — unlikely as Robert had always considered these public function rooms boring with their restrictions and need for polite behaviour. Mr Adam's room? Of course, Robert had had the opportunity to search in there when sent on that convenient errand for the orange. Who knew what he might have spotted and considered useful for a budding sea captain?

How foolish she was. She should have said nothing to Robert about her plans. Or at least given him more hope. Having come this far, there was no way he would retrace his steps with his elder sister. She flung open the door and was through it, forgetting caution.

'Yes? What is the matter?' Mr Adam had been hidden by the bed curtains as he bent to take a book from the table by the window. She stared at him. What was he doing here at this time of day?

He should be in one of the offices, surely.

'Nothing,' she said quickly. 'Nothing at all. I was going to dust. I thought you would be remaining downstairs.'

With one swift stride, he had grasped her hand. 'You have dusted this room within an inch of existence already. And where is your duster? Come — I can tell by your face that something is wrong. How could I not, when you mean so much to me?'

'You are quite mistaken. Perhaps you do not know me so well after all.' She tried to laugh but the resulting sound was suspiciously like a sob.

'If only you would tell me the problem, I am sure I can help you.'

'No. Please let me go.'

He dropped his hand and she began to slowly walk out of the room.

He was behind her at once. 'Where is your brother? That's it isn't it?'

She turned and looked straight at him. 'In the little room. Where else? Waiting for me.' Surely he would hear the beating of her heart.

He sighed. 'I will always be here for you. Always ready to help, whatever your problem may be. And this will never be dependent on your answer to me tomorrow.'

'May I go now please?'

'Yes, of course.'

She tried to hide her relief. She did not know how long she could have maintained an air of calm — if indeed, she had achieved that at all. 'Thank you.' She must not run with Mr Adam watching her. She walked purposefully but slowly down the stairs and into the kitchen.

'Jenny, I think Robert has run away again. I must go after him.'

'Oh, no.' Jenny's face was shocked. 'If you wait a moment, I am sure Samuel will come with you.'

'No, I must not cause a fuss.' She lowered her voice. 'If anyone else leaves now, it will be too obvious.'

'Don't worry. I shall try and keep Mr Adam and Tobias Henge busy.'

Leonora nodded her thanks and went down to the scullery, taking her old gardening shawl from the cupboard there. She paused a moment to listen for movement in the rest of the house and slid out into the garden and round to the street.

Yes, she had escaped unseen. How long a start did Robert have? Would he have set off immediately, as soon as she had left him? But the interview with Adam had not taken long. If only she had not wasted vital minutes searching the upper floors. But that had made sense at the time.

Robert was young and energetic and could run faster than she could. But once away from the town, surely he would slow to a walk? And he might not think that she would come after him so soon. Oh, it was all 'might' and 'perhaps' and she didn't know anything. She began running a few steps before taking a few at a swift walking pace to give herself time to catch her breath and gaze around, peering in the main at the road ahead. Nothing. No sign of the small figure with his bundle.

At first she was hardly aware of the hoof beats behind her. The road to the port of Eskmouth was well used. Her first instinct should have been to stand aside without even looking up, to allow horse and rider to pass but something made her turn. She gasped in dismay. It was the last person she wanted to see. She recognised the large bay only too well. Blindly she picked up her skirts and ran.

He knew what she had planned. Adam Rigton had worked it out and of course was not going to allow Robert to get away. Not once he had had him within his clutches. Poor Robert, coming unknowingly into the worst possible place with no heed for his own safety. But he had not known how he was endangering himself. It was no good, she thought in despair. She could not run any faster. Each breath was searing her throat. Her heartbeats were pounding almost within her head, in time with her feet on the rutted mud of the road.

Could she make off across the fields? She looked round wildly. But it would gain her nothing. There was nowhere a horse could not follow. And suddenly her foot caught on a stone and the hard ground drove all the breath from her lungs as she fell. She lay there, panting, furious with herself. She was dimly aware of the horse wheeling to a halt above her and the rider throwing himself off, to kneel beside her.

'Lucy, Lucy — are you all right?' Adam was shaking her shoulder.

She felt bruised all over but no time to worry about that now. She must give Robert time to get away and as far as possible. 'I am not Lucy. My name is Leonora.' Perhaps that would distract him.

He laughed. 'Such a beautiful name. But I hardly care what your name is, for it would not alter my feelings for you. Why did you run from me? I only want to help you.'

She winced as dramatically as she could, pulling herself up into a sitting position. 'My ankle — it may be broken! No, please do not touch it. It is so painful . . . ' she gasped.

He ignored her pretence and was running gentle but practiced hands around her foot with no regard for propriety. 'Nothing broken.'

'How do you know?'

'I am of farming stock. I am accustomed to turning my hand to anything.'

'I did not know that. So to be the heir of Sir Francis is a great move upwards. A wonderful opportunity.'

'So it might seem. I took up the law to provide for my mother when she was alive. We lost the farm and had huge debts, through my father's mismanagement.' He spoke quite calmly, with no trace of bitterness. 'I was lucky to gain the patronage of the Earl of Northbury, through a boyhood friendship with my father. He provided me with the means to gain my qualifications and therefore to earn my own living. So I know as well as any how you must feel and the problems you face — and would ease your way wherever possible. But Sir Francis has treated you harshly, I feel.'

She glanced up at him. 'Maybe. He rarely shows kindness to anyone.'

'As I am discovering. Advancement is an unfortunate necessity in this world. I could not refuse Sir Francis' offer and the Earl gave me his blessing. But that does not mean that I will do everything Sir Francis commands. As I told you, I may yet turn him down. Would that make me less of a desirable prospect as a husband for you?'

She had almost forgotten. In her mind the dilemma had been avoided in running away with Robert. She had not intended to be present at Carr House long enough to have to give an answer to him. She glanced up at him, startled, seeing only tenderness in his face. 'No, I don't know. Tomorrow . . . '

'I am sorry. You are quite right. That was our agreement. How are you feeling now? Has the shock of the fall subsided a little?'

'Yes, I am quite well now. Enough to walk back safely, thank you.'

'But what of your brother? I am right, am I not? He has run away from you and towards the sea-bound career he craves?'

Leonora shook her head. 'Oh, I am certain I am making a fuss over nothing. I am an over-anxious sister. I expect he has gone on to stay with a friend of our family. We spoke of it. In . . . er . . . Carlisle.'

He shook his head. 'We both know you think nothing of the sort. He will be making for the nearest port. Come, I will have no arguments.' He swung up into the saddle and leaned down to grasp her arms. 'Up behind me.'

Without thinking, she obeyed him. Following her heart maybe when common sense screamed at her that she must not allow herself to trust this man. Robert's life could be at stake. And yet part of her yearned to believe him.

Nothing in his manner gave an impression of evil or guilt. But it would not, would it? She said, 'Where are we going?'

'As far as Robert might reasonably have reached, on foot. I doubt he will have gained the port of Eskmouth yet. Even so and when he does, there will be a limited number of ships to choose from.'

There was no sign of him, as Adam had half suspected. In spite of his innocence about the ease of achieving his aims, Robert seemed a clever and determined lad. He would be expecting pursuit and was not likely to be caught so easily. Perhaps Adam had been too hasty in bringing Leonora with him — but how could he have kept her away? He would have preferred to search the port on his own; that way he could be more discreet. A young woman in a panic asking for her brother would cause too much remark. It would be all too easy for word to get back to Sir Francis who would no doubt be unable to resist making further trouble for the Mayfield family.

Indeed, Adam already knew that there were two ships belonging to Sir Francis in port at present. He was not at all certain of the wisdom of Robert choosing either. He would prefer to take the boy back safely to Eskthwaite while he made some useful enquiries himself and found a suitable vessel and a good captain. He must think of some way to convince Leonora that her presence was not necessary. Perhaps the truth would be a good starting point — and yet she could be as determined as her brother.

As it happened, it was made easy for him. They were in sight of the port when Leonora called over his shoulder, 'Wait.'

Adam was only too ready to bring his horse to a halt. He said, 'I doubt whether Robert could have come so far in the time. Not on foot.'

She said at once, 'I agree. In fact I am wondering whether he will have come this way at all. I half thought of that before but now I am sure of it.'

'Oh?' Adam said suspiciously. 'And what makes you so sure of that?'

Leonora took a deep breath. This would mean giving away the location of her planned refuge but she must be convincing. If she could get Adam off Robert's trail and send him in the wrong direction, it would be worth it.

She would think of somewhere else where she and Robert could go. Anywhere. Losing themselves in one of the big cities should be easy enough. They could make their way to Liverpool maybe. Robert would accept that.

She said, 'We spoke of going to stay with Lucy — the real Lucy.'

'The maid you are supposed to be? I see.'

'She is living with her new husband. Just off the road to Ireby.' Leonora was twisting and turning her head as she spoke, safely behind Adam's broad back so that she was certain he would not notice. She must remain always alert for

133

Robert on the road. If she saw him, she would say nothing, persuade Adam to drop her at Carr House and hurry back to find Robert and escape with him to Liverpool.

At first this plan pleased her. She was sure it would work and that she could find Robert before Adam did. But as they neared Eskthwaite again with no sign of her brother, she knew this plan too had failed. Where could Robert be? But in whichever direction, she must search alone.

She said, 'If you continue to John Hesket's farm at Ireby, I can stay here in case my brother returns. I will give you directions. He may think better of running away after all, particularly when he gets hungry.'

'You think that likely? He struck me as a very determined young man.'

'Oh, he has run away before. Twice, at least — and came back before the next meal time was due.' Trying to sound easy and confident was proving more and more difficult.

'But you did not take his disappear-
ance calmly. Not this time.'

'I was upset. After the strain of
everything else.'

Adam nodded but after helping her
to the ground, he slid down behind her.
She could have screamed with frustration. She said, 'I thought you were
going to see Lucy and her husband at
Ireby?'

'We will check the house first. I think
I agree with you. If he's there, we must
think what must be done, of course.'

Would she never be rid of him? She
ran in, calling for Jenny but the other
girl almost bumped into her in the hall.

They both spoke at once. 'Has he?'

'Have you?'

She turned to Adam and in spite of
her best efforts was unable to keep the
worry and anguish from her face. 'No.'

'I heard. Do not fear, my love. I will
find him.' And swiftly he was kissing her
again and even in the panic and worry
of the moment, it was what she most
wanted him to do.

Oh, if only . . . All too soon they were apart. He said, 'Stay here and I promise I will bring him to you.'

'If anything happened to him, I could not bear it.' Was he telling the truth? If only she dared trust him.

He said, 'I know how much you care for him. I will find him.' And he was gone in a cloud of dust.

8

Leonora stared after him, wondering if she had done the right thing in sending him in the wrong direction. Should she have accepted his help? Perhaps Adam knew nothing about the vital document. She was almost certain that Sir Francis knew of it and that was why her father had been killed. But would Sir Francis be at all likely to tell anyone else? No. He would want the secret dead and buried. As usual, his commands would be issued with no reason given. Sir Francis was accustomed to unthinking obedience.

That meant that Adam might well not know. But being Sir Francis' heir how would he react when he found out? He had said he would give it all up for her. He had seemed to be telling the truth. But she could not take the risk. The stakes were too high.

Leonora wanted nothing more than to hurry after Robert but knew that she must give Adam time to start on his journey. He would be quite capable of doubling back to make sure she was still here. Besides, there was something else she must do.

She ran upstairs, thinking that she must hide the document more safely so that Adam would never discover it. She took it from beneath her pillow and stared at it. It had caused so much trouble. Would it not be better to destroy it now? Burn it? But if Sir Francis knew of its existence, he would keep searching. Should she return it to Sir Francis? She could promise that nothing would be done by she or Robert to jeopardise his position. But being so ruthless and untrustworthy himself, he would not believe her. And, even more dangerous, he would then have proof that she knew his secret.

She stared around the one-time nursery. Yes — the loose floorboard where they had all stored childish treasures. Quickly she moved aside the red and blue rag-rug and her fingers found the nick in the board to lift it out. She stuffed the documents in.

And now she must find Robert.

On the landing she almost bumped into a silent figure. Heart lurching, she thought for one joyful, fearful moment that it was Adam. But of course it was Tobias Henge. She recoiled from him. How long had he been there? Had he seen what she was doing?

He said, 'Ah, Lucy. I was searching for you. I wanted to speak with you.'

'I do not need to speak to you.' She tried to get past him.

He seized her arm. 'I think you do.' He smiled which was almost worse than the implied threat. 'Why the hurry? I think you will welcome what I have to tell you. Are you not looking for someone?'

She felt her face pale. 'No. Why do you think that?'

'There is no use in your denying it. I make it my business to know everything that happens here. That is my job and why Sir Francis employs me. But sometimes I turn my hand to helping ordinary folk. And I am very inclined to help you because I like you, sweet Lucy. So when I saw that your brother needed assistance, I did not turn him away.'

'What? My brother? Do you mean you know where he is?'

'Of course. And I can take you to him. To wish him a sisterly farewell.'

'What do you mean?'

'Why, I have found him a ship and a captain who will take him on. This is what you both wanted, is it not?'

'Well, yes.' She tried to think over what he was telling her. Had she misjudged the sinister clerk? If true, this could be the answer to all their problems. 'But I would certainly like to meet this captain myself. Is he a decent, honest man?'

'Of course. And there is nothing easier than that you should meet Captain Gibbs and decide for yourself. A wise precaution.'

Her father had always said she was too quick too judge, she thought remorsefully. Was Tobias Henge yet another victim of her hastiness because of his unfortunate slimy voice and repulsive manner? Neither of these could be helped, she supposed.

He said, 'I am afraid you will have to make haste if you are to see Master Robert before the ship sails. He is very much looking forward to the venture and his new life but will be disappointed if he does not see you first. Being without parents as he is, you are all he has.'

'Yes, I know.' She must go. She could leave word with Jenny after all.

'Ah, I nearly forgot. Permit me — Master Robert sent a token to show you. 'Leo always argues and fusses,' he said, 'and this will prove you come from me.'' He felt in his pocket and brought out a small bone carving of a ship.

Leonora recognised it at once as he pressed it into her hand. 'Oh! That is Robert's lucky charm.'

'Indeed. He said you would know it. And is relying on you to bring it back so he will not have to set off without it.'

'Of course I will come. He must have it back.' But almost as much as the charm's presence, Henge's words rang true. Even the tone of voice he had hit exactly. 'Leo always argues and fusses.' That was so like Robert.

'Yes, I will come. I will just leave word with Jenny.'

Tobias Henge laughed. 'For whose benefit? Since your employer is dismissing you, he is hardly likely to concern himself what you do.'

Little he knew. Something at least seemed to have escaped Tobias Henge's vigilance. Apparently he had not noticed the growing intensity of feeling between Leonora and Adam.

But there was no need to worry about that now. And once she had seen Robert safely off on his way and out of Adam's and Sir Francis' reach, there would be no need to worry further. Yes, she must trust Tobias at least in this.

There was no alternative.

In spite of his objections, she went into the kitchen to explain. Jenny's look of horror made her uneasy but all the more determined. 'You are never trusting yourself with him, miss! I can't let you.'

'I must. He told me he knows where Robert is. I have to believe him.'

Jenny stared around the kitchen as if seeking inspiration in the row of bright copper pans to where the manservant was aimlessly shuffling plates. 'Samuel! At least take Samuel with you. If Tobias Henge objects you will know he means ill.'

'No, I cannot drag you with us, Samuel. You have duties here.'

'Nothing that matters now, miss,' Samuel mumbled.

'Indeed not,' Jenny said firmly. 'We owe Mr Adam and his employer no loyalty, as he was eager to make all too clear to us. Samuel will keep watch on you and bring word here if needed.'

Yes, that made sense, Leonora

admitted. And a relief to have an old and dear friend with her; someone she knew she could depend upon.

Tobias Henge had arranged that he would drive the light cart from the farm. 'Old Misery there wasn't too keen so near dark but when I said it was for you, he gave in.'

For me? She couldn't think how the farmer would know she was here. Suddenly she realised what Tobias Henge must mean. Of course, the farmer thought the cart was for Lucy. So she had Lucy's cheerful friendliness to thank for this as well as everything else.

They set off briskly but it was almost dark by the time the port came into view. So Robert had been here already all the time she and Adam had been on the road. She should not have allowed Adam to talk her out of carrying onwards. No, that was hardly fair — she had encouraged him to turn back in order to get rid of him and continue alone.

They pulled up near the harbour. Already the surrounding inns were full with noisy crowds, men spilling out onto the narrow cobbled streets, laughing and shouting and not without a rowdy scuffle or two.

'Not a place for a lady,' Samuel muttered.

'Which ship is it?' Leonora hoped Henge had not noticed Samuel's criticism. She wanted no obstacles put in her way, not now she was so near to seeing Robert safe.

'There, see. If you watch the horse and cart, Samuel — they may not still be here for us otherwise and Old Misery at the farm would have something to say. Not that I care much for him,' Tobias Henge chuckled.

Maybe she had not been so far wrong about him after all. His laugh was as unpleasant as ever. But if he could lead her to Robert . . . All the same, she was glad that Samuel was here.

'Come on,' Henge snapped. 'Hurry up.'

She was on fire to see Robert but had the sense of caution to touch Samuel's arm. 'I will be back shortly to travel home with you. I shall make my farewells brief.' Even with Samuel in attendance, the noise and clamour on the quayside made her feel uneasy about the horse and cart. Samuel was beset by a fit of coughing. But no matter. She did not need to hear his reply.

'It's this one, near at hand,' Tobias said. Leonora looked up at the vessel for the first time. The brooding masts were silhouetted against the darkening sky. There was no sign of life on board. But if this was where Robert had chosen to fulfil his ambition then she must be glad for him. Tobias Henge took her arm and hurried her up the gangway.

She said, 'What is the name of this ship, Tobias?'

'Why, The Bright Endeavour.'

Leonora frowned. As they went on board, she was thinking always about

Robert and looking around, seeking a glimpse of him. She would have expected him to be on deck to greet her. But the name seemed familiar. An alarm was sounding at the back of her mind. The decks were clean, obviously the planks had been newly swilled which was good to see but all the same, she seemed to be assailed by a peculiar smell. The cargo maybe, she thought; what does this ship carry? But there was no time to worry about that now.

'Down here. Mind the ladder. And the passage is narrow.'

'Is Robert not to sleep with the rest of the crew?' She was glad of that. The captain must indeed be a kindly man for with no money or contacts to make Robert a midshipman, there was no advantage to him in allowing Robert this position.

'Oh, all comforts, I assure you. There is the small cabin here, made available by the captain for you to say your farewells in private.'

The door had a key on the outside

which Tobias Henge turned. Even as Leonora was thinking how strange this was, the door was open and her fears assuaged for yes, here was Robert. She held out her arms to him. His face lit up. 'Leo! How are you here? Are you to rescue me?'

She turned to Henge. 'What is this? What has happened?'

He was sneering. 'You wanted the boy and here he is.'

'I don't like this ship, Leo. I want to go home. I promise I'll go to Ireby with you, truly I will.'

And suddenly she knew. The Bright Endeavour belonged to Sir Francis. Half remembered snippets of information came together in her head, making everything clear. 'This is a slave ship!'

'And will be the first to leave port — which was what the young master here requested as I recall. Besides, Captain Gibbs is willing to overlook his youth. Thirteen is the required age for a midshipman.'

Perhaps all was not lost, Leonora

thought. Perhaps they could talk their way out of this. 'I think there has been some mistake. As you see, Robert has changed his mind. I am so sorry that you have gone to all this trouble needlessly.' Henge's expression did not seem very encouraging by the way he was grinning at them. She added, 'If you let us go back, we will make it worth your while. We will see that you are amply rewarded for all your kindly efforts to help us.'

'And with what? Empty words I fear. Make no doubt of it, Miss Leonora, I know who you are and the truth of your circumstances.'

Leonora stared at him. Of course he did. There was no point in not recognising that.

'We will give up all claim to the debt. I know you know about the money owed to us by Sir Francis. I am willing to forget all about it.'

'Oh, I'm sure Sir Francis will be pleased to hear that.' He chuckled. He leaned forward towards them, his narrow face now grimly threatening. 'And everything else? Ah, yes, that is the real question.'

Leonora stared at him, feeling cold. Surely he could not know about the inheritance? Sir Francis would never have taken an underling like Henge into his confidence. 'I do not know what you mean,' she said defiantly.

'I think you do. I keep my eyes and ears open. Young Robert here is the very inconvenient true heir to Sir Francis. More than an heir in fact. His existence could make things difficult; very difficult indeed. And Sir Francis has no intention of relinquishing his power to anyone, still less to a weed of a lad like this.'

Robert was pulling at her sleeve. 'What does he mean? Why is he talking about me like that? He's been doing it ever since we got on the ship.'

'Ssh, Robert,' Leonora said desperately, 'We will give up all claim to that too. I swear it.'

'You will indeed. Because once at

sea, young Robert will be sent straight to the bottom. As soon as convenient and the best way to please Sir Francis, No question of that. And obviously you will be accompanying him; we cannot have you running off to all and sundry with fanciful tales.'

'What about Samuel?' Leonora cried. 'He is waiting for me. If I do not return, he will notify someone. The harbour-master.'

'Ah, Samuel. Yes, of course. Unfortunately I think you will find Samuel is no longer there. He has more loyalty to me than you. Blood always counts for more, you see.'

She stared at him, 'I do not know what you mean.'

'Why, that I am Samuel's son. Have you not noted the resemblance?' He laughed harshly. 'No, you would not. People have always noted that I am very much more like my mother.'

Leonora knew at once that he was telling the truth. Several things had suddenly become clear. 'I did not know

Samuel had ever married.'

'A small detail he forgot to mention, no doubt. My mother and I could have starved for all he cared. When he left us, he said he was going to find work to support us but my mother heard little from him. An occasional sum of money in the first few months and then hardly anything. Not enough for a woman with a small child.'

Leonora gasped in disbelief. 'That does not sound like Samuel. And your poor mother — however did she manage?'

'How does any poor woman manage in that situation? The workhouse. And as the rule was that men and woman must be separated and male children from the age of eight, you can understand that there was no tender loving upbringing for me.'

'That was dreadful.' Leonora was almost forgetting her own dire situation in her distress at the thought of how that child must have suffered.

'I do not need you to feel sorry for

me, Miss Mayfield. As you see I have made my own way in life. But all the time, I intended to find my father — who had conveniently disappeared altogether by the time I grew up. But I always knew I would track him down. And I also knew that he would be useful to me — he feels the guilt of his neglect every time he looks at me. He is that most dangerous of men; well meaning but weak.' He laughed again.

'Unfortunately this most useful character lesson will not benefit you for too long, I'm afraid.' He slammed the door and locked it. They could hear his laughter echoing along the passage.

Leonora screamed after him and pummelled the door with her fists. 'Let us out! Help us, please! Can anyone hear me?'

Her fury spent as quickly as it had arisen, she stood back. There was no point in wasting her effort on useless actions. 'We must think what we are to do, Robert.'

'Yes, you will think of something,

won't you, Leo? You are always so good at thinking.'

She hoped she could fulfil Robert's trust in her. But her first thoughts were filled with sadness at Samuel's betrayal. So much now made sense — how oddly Samuel had behaved when Tobias Henge first arrived. How he had never joined in Leonora's and Jenny's criticisms of the man. How he had failed to warn her of Henge's presence more than once.

But she must not waste precious time on bemoaning what could not be altered. They must somehow get off the ship before it left port. She did not know much about ships but if it had been going with that night's tide she would have expected to see signs of activity on deck. There had been nothing. 'If we only knew when the ship will sail,' she murmured.

'Oh, I know that. I have listened to everything anyone has said. I need to learn everything I can in order to go to sea. But not on this ship. I have changed my mind about that, as I told you. I heard them say they do not have their full crew yet and some of the cargo is yet to arrive too. That is where the captain has gone — to find more men in the taverns when they are too drunk to realise what they are agreeing to. It will be tomorrow at the very earliest, they said.'

She hugged him in relief. 'That was very clever of you, Robert. At least we know we have more time.'

'Yes. We are going to escape, aren't we?'

'Yes, of course we are.' She only wished she knew how.

★   ★   ★

It was almost dark when Adam reached the farm where Lucy now lived. In the urgency of the moment, he had hardly thought what he would say. But as he knocked at the small farm house, he was met by two wary and enquiring faces. Their reaction was hardly surprising at this hour. He said abruptly, 'I am

Adam Rigton, agent for the Carrock estates, living at Carr House. I have been Sir Francis' man but will not be for much longer.'

'Yes, we know you,' John Hesket said. He was a solid dark haired man with an open and trustworthy face.

'What is it?' Lucy cried. She was a young woman who might be inclined to stoutness in later years with a kindly and sensible look. He would have liked her at once even without the loyalty and friendship she had shown to the Mayfield family. 'Has something happened to Miss Leonora?'

No pretence here, he noted. Probably his expression had showed them that something was wrong. 'No — but her brother, Robert has run away. Has he come here? Leonora is worried to distraction.'

The couple looked at each other. 'No, — not as yet. Was he expected to come this way?'

Adam explained. How Leonora had told him that they had spoken of coming here. It seemed even less likely now as he heard the words aloud.

'And of course we would take them in,' Lucy said, 'although we have little enough room and they would find it a squash.'

When Adam mentioned his doubts and Robert's long held dream, she added, 'Oh, he would talk of nothing else. No, you're right. He wouldn't have come in this direction. Not on his own. Not so far from the sea.'

'Thank you,' Adam said. 'So I must get back.' He could hardly keep the despair from his voice.

'Rest yourself here for the night,' Lucy said kindly.

'Aye,' John added. 'You are more than welcome.'

'No, I have to go to her aid.' He shook his head, feeling all the more determined. 'How can I get her to trust me? What can I do? My intentions are to do nothing but help her and yet she has been surrounded by tragedy and she cannot know who to believe. I must

157

go back to the house and prevent her going to the port alone.'

'Wait,' Lucy said. 'My husband will come with you.'

'Indeed, I will,' John said, reaching for his jacket. 'I'll get the horse ready.' He went outside.

Lucy was saying, 'Perhaps she will listen to us. I will tell you frankly, I was ready to dislike you before you came — but the reputation you have earned is for nothing but good. And if I ever saw an honest man, you are he. Miss Leonora needs all the help and friendship she can find.'

In the face of her true and direct stare, Adam found himself saying, 'I wish to offer her more than friendship — if she will have me.'

'Oh, that would be perfect,' Lucy said warmly. 'And I wish you both happiness. And depend upon it, Robert will be warm and snug in someone's barn for now. He got himself to your house safely before and he will do the same again. He's a sensible lad. And Leonora will be waiting where you left her. She won't leave until daylight. Not on her own.'

Adam shook his head. 'It makes sense I know but I cannot rest here knowing how troubled she is. I must go to her.'

John was already calling from the small yard. 'I'm ready. We can be off as soon as you like.'

Adam ran out to where he had tethered his own horse. 'Thank you,' he called over his shoulder. 'For everything.' For trusting me, a stranger, he added silently.

'Never you fear,' John Hesket said. 'We'll find him. The moon will be up soon. Bright as day.'

The return journey could not have taken long but it seemed like hours. If only he were returning to Leonora with good news, Adam thought. At Carr House, Jenny, bless her, was still up with a candle waiting to let him in. 'Mr Adam — have you found him?' Jenny asked.

He shook his head. 'Miss Leonora?' he demanded. 'Where is she? Upstairs?' Strange that she too had not come running at the sound of the horses' hooves.

'She was here,' Jenny said. 'There has been so much coming and going today, I can tell you.'

Was she deliberately seeking to delay him? Or just refusing to tell him anything? Heaven knew that the servants had enough reason not to be obliging after the way he had treated them. But he would put that right; he was resolved on that.

No one stood in his way as he raced up the stairs. That told him more than anything else that searching up here would prove fruitless. Below him, he could hear Jenny speaking to Lucy's husband, obviously surprised to see him. Perhaps John would convince her that he could be trusted.

He flung open the door of Leonora and Jenny's room. A packed bundle was ready on one of the beds and evidence of the beginnings of packing on the other. So Leonora had not yet left permanently; that was something. How little the servants possessed. He must assume that the few items of clothing on the bed near the window belonged to Jenny. And this would be Leonora's; he turned from one to the other, hoping foolishly to draw some conclusion as to what her actions may have been and almost fell as he caught his foot in the rug.

He cursed his own foolishness and tried to straighten the rug with his foot, not wanting either of the girls to fall. No, even now the floor was still uneven. It was caused by the boards underneath. He must get Samuel onto making them more level.

He kicked the rug out of the way completely. If he had not been so achingly aware of anything to do with Leonora he might never have noticed one board in particular. It was at least an inch out of place, as if someone had lifted it recently. And of course, Robert had been up here on his own for some time and might easily have decided to retrieve some treasured item. He'd had a similar hiding hole in his own room as a boy. Adam smiled briefly at the memory.

An idea came to him. If Robert had used this as a hiding place, then so had Leonora and her sister. He lifted the board and yes, the space was almost filled with small boxes and bundles and a wooden ship and a doll without eyes. And on top, laid there with haste he would guess, were two official looking documents.

Heart beating in rapid excitement, he pulled them out and began to read. He finished and sat for a moment with clenched fists, head bowed before striding onto the landing and calling down to John. 'Quickly, if you would. There is something important I need you to do.'

9

Leonora listened, her ear pressed to the door. The ship seemed quiet still although bursts of drunken laughter still wafted over from the harbour. There was no window in their small space but judging by the direction of the sounds and the gentle noise of lapping water, she assumed they must be on the seaward side. A pity. If Samuel had still been there, she might have attracted his attention. Surely he would remember old ties of loyalty and friendship if she appealed to him directly? As she had grown up, he had always been more of a friend than a servant, always ready to join in her games. But who knew the depth of Henge's hold over his father?

But appealing to Samuel had to be a risk worth taking if they could get on deck and he was still in sight. And surely if the ship was still at the quayside, getting to the shore would not prove too much of a problem. First, however, they must escape from the cabin.

'How long do they mean to keep us here?' she muttered to herself. 'Will they feed us? Is anyone on guard outside?' She rattled the door handle. Sir Francis' ship, whatever its unsavoury purpose, was well built of stout oak. She thought she could hear a chuckle. She called softly, 'Mr Henge? Is anyone there?'

No answer at first, merely a scuffling which could have been rats. She would have to think of something else. And then that hated, leering voice. 'I'm always here, Miss Mayfield. And shall be until my orders are finally carried out. Don't you worry about that.'

A rat after all, though a human one. 'And what might those orders be?' Keep him talking; she was not sure where this would lead but anything was better than nothing at all.

'I believe I have made them clear to you already. Have you forgotten so soon? If that is the case, the surprise will be all the sweeter.' He laughed as they heard his footsteps moving away. Another of his tricks; no doubt he wanted to encourage her at useless banging and rattling of the door, all for his own wicked amusement.

'We can search the cabin,' Robert whispered. 'There may be a secret door or a loose panel.'

Yes, they might as well. But even with an eager Robert assisting, their finger tips found nothing that would easily fall apart to help them.

Try something else. 'Has anyone been in at all since you arrived, Robert? Have you been given anything to eat or drink?'

'Yes. I banged on the door and said I was hungry. It was only biscuits,' Robert said seriously. 'Very hard but I am ready to get used to that. It is what seamen always eat.'

Leonora closed her eyes briefly with relief. They would hardly trouble to feed them if they were going to dispose of them soon. 'Who brought it? Did he seem friendly?'

'Not really. He laughed but not in a friendly way. He said Mr Henge had given orders that only he himself was to tend to me but he'd gone off on his own business and this wasn't his ship. So if Gabriel Long chose to feed the prisoner that was up to him. I don't think he was being kind to me, Leo. I think he was doing it to spite Tobias.'

A pity that Tobias had returned in that case. This Gabriel Long might have been promising.

Robert sneezed. She glanced at him. He said, 'it's all right, Leo. Only the dust. I shall get accustomed to that.'

But that had given her an idea. Yes, it was worth a try. She glanced around the cabin — not much that would help her but there was a small three-legged stool. She whispered quickly to Robert and banged on the door, trying to make her voice panic stricken. 'Mr Henge! My brother is feverish. It is airless in here. If we could go up on deck for a little air?'

'Not possible.'

'A drink at least. And some water to bathe his forehead. I beg you!' She turned to smile encouragement to Robert and gave a little scream. A genuine reaction as Robert had collapsed onto the bunk with his eyes rolled back in his head. A trick that had sent his nurse and his sisters into hysterics on many an occasion, however often he was punished for it. 'Oh, no!'

'What's the matter in there?' It sounded as if Tobias Henge was beginning to be convinced.

'It is his old trouble; the doctor always said it might prove fatal one day.' She bit her lip. Was she overdoing this? If Sir Francis wanted Robert out of the way, an early death from natural causes would be all to the good.

But no. Tobias Henge was unlocking the door. 'I need for Sir Francis to see him first,' he muttered. 'Else I'll not get paid for it. Those were my instructions.

Lest there be any mistakes.'

'There — see!' Leonora pointed to the bunk as, right on cue, Robert gave a strangled gurgle.

Tobias Henge leaned over him. 'What ails the lad? Some kind of fit?'

Leonora swung the stool upwards and brought it down on his head. Robert wriggled away as Henge fell forwards. 'Have you killed him? Well done, Leo.'

She was shaking. 'I hope not. Just enough to knock him out. While we escape.' No, he was still breathing, thank goodness. She was weak with relief. 'Come, Robert.'

She took his hand and they ran up onto the deserted deck.

Or the deck which had been deserted only moments before. Now, there was a dark coach drawn up on the quayside and figures ascending the gangway. 'Ah, Miss Mayfield.' It was the steely voice of Sir Francis. 'We meet once more.'

★ ★ ★

Leonora said calmly, although inwardly she was cold with fear, 'We were just about to leave.'

'I think not.' Sir Francis gestured to one of the men accompanying him. 'Go and see what the redoubtable Miss Mayfield has done to the servant set to guard her. Although on this poor showing, he will not be my servant for much longer.'

He turned to face Leonora and Robert, elegant in his blood red velvet, his face as bored as if discussing an outing to Vauxhall. 'No, you wished to go to sea and so you shall. I have been intending to visit my plantations, to oversee the whole trading process which has not been overly efficient of late. We shall go together, Miss Mayfield — and Master Mayfield? It will be most pleasant, I'm sure.'

Leonora felt an instant of hope. Had Tobias Henge been acting alone in his plan to dispose of them? She had always felt that Sir Francis would not be willing to actually witness any villainy he set in train.

She said, 'That is most kind, I am sure, but I do not feel it appropriate for my brother to have his first experience at sea on a slave ship. And it was never my own intention to go to sea at all,' she said as steadily as possible.

He smiled and she knew that she and Robert were in the greatest danger they had ever been. 'Be assured that you will see neither hide nor hair of any slave. The first leg of the journey is to the coast of Africa — only then do the new slaves come aboard and by then, your voyage will be long over.'

From the corner of her eye and out of Sir Francis' vision, she became aware of movement on the quayside — an eerily soundless scuffle was progressing. She dared not look directly or allow the hope to show in her face. She squeezed Robert's hand tightly, willing him to understand.

'Ow, Leo,' Robert said loudly. 'I know you are frightened but there is no need to squash my hand like that. There is nothing to fear now that we are safely in Sir Francis' hands. And I will always look after you.' He was trying to draw attention to himself, Leonora realised. He understood everything. But they needed something more.

Perhaps if a small diversion might be arranged? She edged round so that, to continue looking at her, Sir Francis must face the sea. The ship's rail was not high. Beyond it, she could see that the waves were no longer lapping placidly but were becoming choppy. Swiftly she turned, grasped the rail and began to scramble over, pulling Robert with her. She did not want to jump but would if she had to.

But no, all was happening as she had hoped. Sir Francis swore, issued a command and burly arms were pulling her back. No matter, her action had taken all the attention away from the quayside. She only hoped her instincts were right. Robert was now kicking and struggling for good measure. 'Let me go,' he shouted. A hand was clapped-over his mouth.

'No escape that way, I'm afraid,' Sir Francis said.

Leonora swayed, putting a hand to her brow. 'I am sorry. A foolish impulse. I must have misunderstood you. Because what possible reason would you have to harm us?'

'I believe you know only too well. A clever pretence, Miss Mayfield, but not clever enough. Yes, your face betrays you. You cannot deceive me. Your father told you, as all along I suspected he might. A foolish man. He would have been better keeping his mouth shut.'

'He told us nothing.'

'But you know what I am referring to. That is obvious. If you two remain alive, you will be an ever present danger to me. Naturally I cannot allow that. But with you gone and the documents which your father mentioned discov-ered, my problems will be over.'

'You will never find them.' The quay was quiet now. No sound or movement.

Her heart sank. She must have been mistaken. The scuffle must have been drunken revellers after all.

No one was coming. There would be no rescue.

'Well I believe you may be persuaded to tell me where they are. Am I right in thinking that the boy knows nothing of the document or its content?'

Robert wriggled out from his captor's grip. 'I do know. It's the money you owe us. The four thousand pounds. The debt you never repaid my father.'

Sir Francis nodded. 'As I thought. So. I believe I can offer you an agreement. If you tell me where the document is, I will spare your brother.'

Leonora hesitated. Was he telling the truth? Could Sir Francis ever be trusted? And yet if there was a chance that Robert's life might be saved, could she take the risk?

'What use his inheritance,' Sir Francis said softly, stepping forward and grasping her wrist, 'if he is not alive to enjoy it? Be sensible. Tell me.'

No, she did not believe him. But she could not throw away any possibility, however slight, that Robert's life might be spared.

She opened her mouth to reply — and then suddenly the deck was filled with dark clad figures with a familiar form at their head.

'Miss Mayfield cannot tell you, Sir Francis because she does not know.' Adam's expression was grim but as he glanced at her she knew his intention was to reassure her; she read the love in his eyes.

Sir Francis swung round. 'Rigton. Ah — you have found it at last. And you have decided where your interests lie and have brought it to me. Good.'

'I do indeed know where my true interests lie. And they are not with you and your evil game.'

Sir Francis hissed, 'You will suffer for this. Where is it?'

'Where it will do you no good. It is by now lodged with — and will have been read by — the Earl of Northbury.

It has been delivered by a trusted messenger. Furthermore, the Earl will know what steps to take if I do not return to him forthwith.'

Sir Francis staggered, his face drained of blood. 'I do not believe you.'

'It is quite true. Whether you believe me or not is of no consequence.'

'You fool. After I was intending to make you my heir — by your actions you will lose everything I promised you.'

'That was at the cost of my integrity. That price would always have been too high to pay.'

'Seize him!' Sir Francis shouted. But the men now crowding across the deck were not the down at heel sailors he expected to see. They were a mixture of farmhands with stout cudgels and a group of other men equally well armed who might be servants.

Adam said, 'Your men have been dealt with on shore. But there is no need to worry about them; they will be ready to sail eventually — although with somewhat sore heads.' He stretched out his hand. 'Miss Mayfield? May I escort you home?'

She kept her eyes on Adam's face, not wanting to look at Sir Francis, ever again. But Robert, remembering his manners, paused and bowed. 'Good day to you, Sir Francis. I am indeed sorry not to be sailing with you after all but I believe the position would not have suited me,' he said.

'Get away from me, you stupid brat. And you, Rigton, are no longer in my employ. You will leave Carr House at once.'

'Certainly. It is what we had intended. We will go at once and seek refuge with the Earl who is well able to protect us.'

'You had best watch your backs,' Sir Francis growled. 'And I will see to it that no one else will employ you. I have many contacts. And that will just be the beginning.'

'As I said, the Earl is expecting us. If we should fail to arrive, he will know who to blame, so you had better hope that we arrive safely.'

He proffered his arm and Leonora swept off the ship as well as she was able, calling to mind every deportment lesson she had ever had. But inside she was shaking. Sir Francis was a man of uncertain temper. Turning her back on him took all her courage.

But as his men left the deck behind and around them, she realised Adam had brought a veritable army. Some of the men she recognised from Town End farm; some were in a discreet grey livery unknown to her. Their presence was reassuring but more than anything, she had to feel safe now with the man she loved by her side.

He was saying, 'Can you ride behind me? And Robert with Samuel? It will be quicker.'

'Samuel!' Leonora cried. 'You came back.'

'Indeed, miss. I had to,' he said. 'I met Mr Adam on the road. Can you ever forgive me?'

'Of course. Henge is your son, after all.'

'I had to do my best for him. I was torn. But I don't know what lies he may have told you about our circumstances.'

'It doesn't matter. I am sure you did what you could for him and his mother at the time.'

'My wife left me for another man, named Henge, taking our small son with her. I never saw either of them until Tobias came up here to work for Sir Francis. I told him to keep his distance at first but when he turned up on your doorstep, what could I do?'

Leonora felt that explained a great deal. Poor Samuel. Why had she been willing to believe Tobias Henge without hearing Samuel's side? But no matter. All she wanted to do now was to cling to the safety of Adam's broad back but Robert was saying cheerfully as they set off, 'I thought Sir Francis was going to explode. He went very red. Didn't you think so?'

Adam laughed. Leonora said, 'I didn't actually look. I hope I never have to see him again.'

Adam said, turning his head, 'He will fight the claim. No doubt about that. But I can arrange all that for you. If you will allow me to?'

She smiled up at him. 'I am sure my father never wished to supplant Sir Francis. All he would have wanted was for Robert to have the right to succeed him. We do not care for the Carrock estates. All I want is to be together with Robert and Sophy.' She smiled. 'And with you.'

Her last words were swept away by the rising wind. She must hope that her eyes had spoken her thought. By the look of Adam's smile, she knew that he understood.

He turned away and shouted across to Samuel, 'There is bad weather coming with the dawn. We must ride.'

10

They arrived safely at Northbury Place, although weary and soaked to the skin. A long ride, into the neighbouring county, and the countryside was assailed by a fierce band of storms. The weather however, was in complete contrast to the warmth of their welcome. They were swept into the care of the kindly housekeeper with much head shaking and small cries of concern.

When the week of storms finally ceased, Adam had no qualms about leaving them there — although he had intended setting off without Leonora knowing. A forlorn hope; they were both aware of the other's movements; she seemed to have an instinct for his possible danger. She appeared in the stable yard as he was mounting his horse. 'Where are you going?'

He would tell her part of it at least.

'Back to Carr House. To collect what possessions of yours are still there, while I may.'

'Yes, I would be very grateful. Lady Northbury has been so kind — indeed the whole household — but I cannot keep borrowing. Wait a few moments and I will come with you.'

'No. I do not know what I might find,' he said frankly. 'There is a possibility that Sir Francis might have given instructions about anyone returning to the house.'

'Then you must not go either, if there is danger.'

'My possessions are there too. I promise you if I see anything to cause unease I will return here and only go back with some of the Earl's men with me. But for now, on my own, I can easily escape notice.'

It made sense, Leonora supposed. 'If necessary, you can go along the river bank into the back garden.' The secret way they had learned as children. The route Lucy had taken as she left to marry John; it seemed months ago now rather than merely weeks.

* * *

Leonora missed Adam more than she would have thought possible. For so long now, he had been under the same roof. And because of that and although it had been a testing and difficult time, she thought of those weeks with regret. If only she had realised sooner how she felt about him. They had wasted so much time. Now every hour they were apart was too long.

On the fourth day however, she saw his horse on the sweep of the drive and regardless of all propriety, ran out to greet him.

Her face was alight with joy. 'Oh, Adam. I thought something had happened to you.'

He flung himself from his horse and drew her close. 'Never. Not when I knew that you were waiting here for me.'

She threw her arms around his neck. 'I was so fearful for you. Sir Francis can be so dangerous when crossed. And there is Henge too.'

'Indeed. I did not tell you but I was concerned about Henge most of all. Knowing he must have killed your father to please Sir Francis and would stop at nothing. So I did not stop long at Carr House but continued to Eskmouth to find out.'

'Adam, that was foolish. If I had known you were to dive into the hornet's nest like that, I would have stopped you. How could you?'

He laughed. 'It was fortunate, then, that you did not know. But I have news. Sir Francis insisted that they should sail as planned, although against his captain's advice and with the storms ready to break at any moment. Apparently he said that he would not employ a captain who was afraid of a bit of a wind.'

He paused, his voice sombre. 'The Bright Endeavour went down, Leonora. There is no doubt. It was witnessed

183

from the shore.'

Her face clouded. 'Did anyone survive?'

'None. Both Sir Francis and Tobias Henge are gone. You will never be troubled by them again.'

'I would not wish such an end on anyone, but they were responsible for my dear father's death so justice has been done.' She smiled up at him.

Adam said, 'Indeed it has. And now with all thought of danger past, we can send for Sophy and all look to the future together.' His voice was tender. 'A future that I would wish for you and I to be able to share. I could not exist without you.'

'Adam!' It was Robert's voice. 'You're back. Can I go to sea now?'

Adam laughed. 'I am sure something can be arranged. But would you not like to stay for your sister's wedding first?'

'Not much. But I suppose I'll have to.'

'You certainly will.'

She hardly noticed Robert's rapid steps as he raced away, for at last Adam was kissing her and they had all the time in the world.

THE END